Emily Harvale lives in]
– although she would prefer to live in the French Alps ... or Canada ... or anywhere that has several months of snow. Emily loves snow almost as much as she loves Christmas.

Having worked in the City (London) for several years, Emily returned to her home town of Hastings where she spends her days writing ... and wondering if it will ever snow.

You can contact her via her website, Facebook or Instagram.

There is also a Facebook group where fans can chat with Emily about her books, her writing day and life in general. Details can be found on Emily's website.

Author contacts:
www.emilyharvale.com
www.twitter.com/emilyharvale
www.facebook.com/emilyharvalewriter
www.instagram.com/emilyharvale

***

Scan the code above to see all Emily's books on Amazon

Also by this author

The Golf Widows' Club
Sailing Solo
Carole Singer's Christmas
Christmas Wishes
A Slippery Slope
The Perfect Christmas Plan
Be Mine
It Takes Two
Bells and Bows on Mistletoe Row

Lizzie Marshall series:
Highland Fling – book 1
Lizzie Marshall's Wedding – book 2

Goldebury Bay series:
Ninety Days of Summer – book 1
Ninety Steps to Summerhill – book 2
Ninety Days to Christmas – book 3

Hideaway Down series:
A Christmas Hideaway – book 1
Catch A Falling Star – book 2
Walking on Sunshine – book 3
Dancing in the Rain – book 4

Hall's Cross series
Deck the Halls – book 1
The Starlight Ball – book 2

Michaelmas Bay series
Christmas Secrets in Snowflake Cove – book 1
Blame it on the Moonlight – book 2

Lily Pond Lane series
The Cottage on Lily Pond Lane – four-part serial
Part One – New beginnings
Part Two – Summer secrets
Part Three – Autumn leaves

Part Four – Trick or treat
Christmas on Lily Pond Lane
Return to Lily Pond Lane
A Wedding on Lily Pond Lane
Secret Wishes and Summer Kisses on Lily Pond Lane

Wyntersleap series
Christmas at Wynter House – Book 1
New Beginnings at Wynter House – Book 2
A Wedding at Wynter House – Book 3
Love is in the Air – spin off

Merriment Bay series
Coming Home to Merriment Bay – Book 1
(four-part serial)
Part One – A Reunion
Part Two – Sparks Fly
Part Three – Christmas
Part Four – Starry Skies
Chasing Moonbeams in Merriment Bay – Book 2
Wedding Bells in Merriment Bay – Book 3

Seahorse Harbour series
Summer at my Sister's – book 1
Christmas at Aunt Elsie's – book 2
Just for Christmas – book 3
Tasty Treats at Seahorse Bites Café – book 4
Dreams and Schemes at The Seahorse Inn – book 5
Weddings and Reunions in Seahorse Harbour – book 6

Clementine Cove series
Christmas at Clementine Cove – book 1
Broken Hearts and Fresh Starts at Cove Café – book 2
Friendships Blossom in Clementine Cove – book 3

Norman Landing series
Saving Christmas – book 1
A not so secret Winter Wedding – book 2
Sunsets and surprises at Seascape Café-book 3
A Date at the end of The Pier – book 4

ISBN 978-1-917227-04-9

Published by Crescent Gate Publishing

Print edition published worldwide 2024
E-edition published worldwide 2024

Cover design by JR and Emily Harvale

Acknowledgements

My grateful thanks go to the following:

My webmaster, David Cleworth who does so much more than website stuff.
My cover design team, JR.
Luke Brabants. Luke is a talented artist and can be found at: www.lukebrabants.com
My wonderful friends for their friendship and love. You know I love you all.
All the fabulous members of my Readers' Club. You help and support me in so many ways and I am truly grateful for your ongoing friendship. I wouldn't be where I am today without you.
My Twitter and Facebook friends, and fans of my Facebook author page. It's great to chat with you. You help to keep me (relatively) sane!

To the wonderful members of my Facebook group, and to my equally wonderful, newsletter subscribers. This book is also dedicated to one of those people in particular; the winner of a competition to have a character named after them.
The winner was Madeline Barnfather, also known as Madi, and the character in this book is Madi, Noelle's best friend.

Emily Harvale

Christmas on Midwinter Lane

CRESCENT GATE PUBLISHING

One

'A pinch and a punch for the first of the month. Good morning!'

I had answered my phone, having seen it was my best friend, Madi, calling, and despite being in the middle of a mini crisis, I smiled on hearing her cheery voice.

'A slap and a kick for being so quick,' I replied. 'Good morning to you too. Although to be honest, it isn't such a good morning here.'

'Oh no. What's wrong?' The concern in Madi's voice was genuine.

'The heating's playing up. I'm in the utility room right now and I believe I've fixed it temporarily. I checked the boiler and the pilot light was lit, so I googled what, if anything, I could do, and it said to turn the boiler off, wait for thirty seconds and then turn it back on again, so that's what I did. And, hey presto, the heating burst into life about a minute ago. But according to the internet searches I made, I think that means either the thermostat or the programmer is faulty. Which means I'll have to call out a heating engineer. And today's Sunday, so that's not good either. But hey ho. Such is life.'

'That's not good, you're right,' Madi agreed. 'Especially not on your anniversary.'

'Luckily,' I said, 'I have this lovely, thick and cosy dressing gown you bought me last Christmas, to help keep out the freezing cold. But it's a shame it happened on my anniversary, I agree, and it's not a great start to my favourite month of the year. Still, ...' I added bleakly. 'I suppose things could've been worse.'

Madi and I were referring to the anniversary of the day I moved into my cottage. Exactly one year ago today, the first of December.

I had grown up in the nearby seaside town of Fairlight Bay and had often admired the row of three cottages that stood on Midwinter Ridge, the group of hills that rose behind the town sheltering it from the worst of the winter winds from the North. As a child, I wondered who had decided to build a row of just three cottages and on such a high and exposed place, away from the town. Dad told me they were farm cottages, rebuilt in the early 1800s to replace the original but much smaller 'hovels' that had stood there since the Middle Ages, and that all the land as far as the eye could see had once been part of the extensive and ancient, Midwinter Farm. These days, the farm consisted of a few fields of sheep and cows, some chickens and ducks, and an Elizabethan Farmhouse, that had also replaced the original farmhouse, but that was now far too grand for what was little more than a smallholding.

I never expected to live in one of those cottages myself, and when I was twenty-one, I moved from my parents' house, and away from Fairlight Bay to pursue a career in London.

When I decided to return to my hometown, as I had always thought of it, I saw one of the cottages up on Midwinter Ridge was on the market, and I immediately made an offer. I moved into the aptly, if somewhat boringly named, Middle Cottage (it being the middle of the row of three) on Midwinter Lane last December. The other cottages being End Cottage, to the left of mine, and Far Cottage, to the right. Oh, how I would've loved to meet the person who had decided on those names! I would've given them a few tips on using their imagination.

The day I moved in was a bitterly cold day, just like this one, but unlike today, the sun shone and the clear sky was an icy blue.

Today the sky was gunmetal-grey and there was no sign of the sun. Although to be fair, it wasn't due to rise for another ten minutes.

'I can't believe you've been there for a year,' Madi added.

'Neither can I. It's absolutely flown.'

I clamped my phone between my shoulder and my ear and adjusted my dressing gown, tying the belt tighter to keep out the chill of the December morning air.

The cottage was usually warm and cosy by this time in the morning; the timer being set for the heating to come on at exactly five-thirty each day, including Sundays, when most people I knew had a lie-in. But when I awoke this morning, just before seven, having overslept for the first time in months, my bedroom – and I had correctly assumed, the rest of the cottage, was as cold as the bedrooms in the Ice Hotel in Sweden.

Not that I'd been to the Ice Hotle in Sweden. Or to any hotel made of ice, so I couldn't say for sure, but Madi and I had watched a documentary about it and how they built it from scratch each year. We had promptly added, 'spend a night in an Ice Hotel' to our respective lists of 'Things I should do before my hair turns grey.' Our lists were so similar, that we could've had just one list. We had both squeezed it in between 'see the Northern Lights' and 'go on a husky drawn sleigh ride'.

Spending the night – and no doubt a fortune – to stay in sub-zero temperatures seemed like a worthwhile and rather thrilling experience when I had added it to my list. Waking up in my own freezing bedroom this morning, was another thing entirely. And not at all thrilling.

Normally, I had showered and dressed long before seven-thirty, but not wanting to leave the warmth of my cosy bed, I had remained curled up beneath the duvet for almost fifteen minutes. The temptation to stay there all morning was strong, but I had places to go, and people to see, so I had no choice but to brave the cold.

I hurried to the utility room half expecting to find the boiler had completely given up the ghost, but thankfully, there still seemed to be life in the old thing, and having discovered how to resolve the problem – albeit temporarily, I had heating once again.

'It's great that you managed to get it working,' Madi said. 'Things can only get better from here. But you don't sound like your usual cheery self. Is everything else okay?'

I snuggled my neck into the deep collar of my dressing gown as I removed the phone from beneath my chin and held it in my hand.

'Apart from the fact that this place is freezing, and polar bears would feel at home here, you mean? I think there's actually ice on the *inside* of my windows!'

I laughed as I padded from the small utility room into the kitchen of my bone-tinglingly cold cottage, grateful not only for the cosy dressing gown but also for my furry, slipper boots, shaped like reindeer heads. Each one had hand stitched eyes and a grinning mouth between which there was a plastic nose that lit up with each step I took. Or every move I made if I was sitting down, or sprawled out length-wise on the sofa. I bought them as a present for myself from the Christmas Market in town last year, and I loved them so much that I bought some for Madi, and also for my mum. Madi loved them too. Mum, not so much.

'Oh!' Mum had said when she opened her present on Christmas morning. 'Are these for me?' And when I nodded in the affirmative, she gave me an odd look, glanced at my dad, who shrugged, and then with a smile as false as Gran's teeth, added, 'How lovely.'

Luckily, I had also bought Mum the cardigan I knew she wanted, so it wasn't a complete disaster. Gran pinched the slippers when neither of us were looking and she's apparently been wearing them every day since, even in the summer.

I placed my phone on the counter and pressed the speaker icon so that I could continue the conversation with Madi while I filled the kettle. I was dying for a mug of steaming hot coffee, partly to warm up my hands, but mainly because I needed the caffeine rush.

'Yeah. Apart from that.' Madi laughed.

I let out a small sigh as I switched on the kettle. 'Yeah. Everything's great. Except I overslept, and I think I may have a teensy, weensy hangover. Foolishly, I joined Berry for – to use her exact words, "one quick drink in The Dog and Duck." Four hours and at least six large red wines later, I can't remember how I got home. I believe Paul might've carried me from his car, but I must've got myself to bed ... at least I hope I did. I was wearing my PJs when I woke up, and the top was on back to front, so ...' I gave a little shrug even though Madi couldn't see me, 'somehow I got undressed.'

Madi gurgled with laughter. She had only met my new friend, Berenice, or Berry, as she liked to be called, a few times, but that was enough for Madi to size her up and agree that Berry was our kind of friend. Paul was Berry's older brother, and as Madi had said when she met him, he was "Hot as hell and twice as sexy." He had a girlfriend, though, so that was a bit of a downer, as Madi and I had agreed, but as Madi had also said, "Girlfriends don't always last."

'Maybe Paul undressed you,' said Madi in a wistful tone. 'He could undress me anytime. If I wasn't happily engaged to the love of my life, that is,' she added hastily. 'He's still with his girlfriend, I assume?'

'Sadly for me, yes. But enough about me. Everything okay with you? This is an early call even by your standards. You usually sleep in on a Sunday.'

Madi and I chatted almost every day, and Madi often called at around eight in the morning, except on a Sunday. Sunday was the one day of the week that she liked to sleep late.

Madi was an early bird and had been for the fifteen years I had known her. I was more of a night owl, although since moving into Middle Cottage, my habits, and my entire life, had changed. These days, I was usually up and about long before the lark had even opened its eyes, let alone started singing.

Not that the tiny hamlet of Midwinter had an abundance of larks. In fact, I had never seen one. Sparrows, magpies, blackbirds, collared doves and, of course, my favourite birds – robins, were plentiful, especially as I had a bird table in my back garden, together with several hanging feeders brimming with seed, suet balls, and so forth.

Swans, geese, ducks, and moorhens were frequent visitors too, often gliding along Midwinter Brook which ran close by the row of three cottages on Midwinter Lane, and was a tributary of Midwinter River. The river was about two miles away and cascaded down one side of Midwinter Ridge, then flowed past Midwinter Farm, before it curved back around the foot of the hills and made its way through Fairlight Glen, a beautiful area of woodland and shrubs. From there the river skirted the town of Fairlight Bay, as it made its way to the sea.

There were partridges, too. Sadly, not in pear trees – which would be lovely at this time of the year – but scurrying across the fields that surrounded the cottages, and weaving in and out of the hedgerows that were bursting with winter berries, separating the cottages and the fields.

Sheep and cows grazed in those fields in summer; the grass strewn with wild flowers loved by butterflies, birds, and bees, but this time of year, the cows were in their sheds, and although the sheep remained outside for most of the winter except for when the fields were sodden, or the weather was too grim, they preferred to be closer to the farmhouse down in the valley on the other side of

Midwinter Ridge rather than up on the exposed hills.

The hills that formed Midwinter Ridge were also known locally as the fire hills. This was because of the proliferation of wild gorse bushes that grew on the sides of the hills facing the sea. In the spring, when the gorse bushes were covered in a blanket of yellow-gold blooms, the hills gave the appearance of being on fire.

'All good here, thanks,' said Madi. 'And nothing much to report, apart from that the weather's naff, so I'm going to have a lazy day by the fire. What about you? Got any exciting plans for the day? I just wanted to be the first one to wish you a jolly December. And speaking of jolly, how are the two grinches?'

Madi meant my two neighbours, Adele, and Marcus, who lived in the cottages either side of mine. When I moved into Middle Cottage last December, not only had my neighbours kept themselves to themselves, they hadn't put up any decorations – at least, none that I could see. Both Madi and I adored Christmas, although me more so than Madi, so the lack of decorations was an afront to our senses and we'd been discussing it ever since.

My boxes of Christmas decorations, of which there were a lot – and I do mean, A LOT – had been the first boxes I had unpacked ... after the box labelled 'kitchen essentials', that is. That box held my kettle, my matching jars containing coffee, teabags, and sugar, another jar brimming with homemade Christmas cookies, and a cooler bag with a three-litre plastic bottle of milk.

Between making the removal team copious cups of coffee and tea, I began putting up my decorations. The removal men even helped. And they complimented me on my delicious Christmas cookies, too.

Once my boxes were unpacked and I had settled in, I had popped round to each cottage to introduce myself but neither neighbour had given me a warm welcome and neither of them had invited me in. Nor had they given me their names, which Madi said was particularly unfriendly.

'Perhaps I caught them both at a bad time,' I had proffered in their defence that day. 'The woman did say she was on the phone, although she didn't have one in her hand when she answered the door. The man just said, "No thanks to whatever it is you're selling", and closed the door in my face.'

'Perhaps you did,' Madi had said, sounding unconvinced. 'But they didn't have to be rude.'

I had tried again but neither neighbour had answered their door, and I had posted Christmas cards through their letterboxes the week before Christmas, but hadn't received cards from them in return.

'Some people don't send cards these days,' I told Madi, trying to hide my disappointment. 'They give to charity instead.' I had decided to give my neighbours the benefit of the doubt. I was sure they had probably done that.

Madi, however, was not convinced.

'I think you're being kind,' she said. 'There aren't any postal costs involved in dropping a card through a neighbour's letterbox, so saving that expense doesn't stack up in my opinion. And buying a pack of charity cards doesn't cost much, and is also giving money to charity, so that's a win-win.'

I couldn't argue with that logic, which made the disappointment greater.

'I think they might just be unfriendly people,' Madi said at New Year, when the neighbours hadn't responded to my invitation to my small, New Year's Eve party. Madi, together with her fiancé, Tristan, had driven all the way from their relatively new home in Somerset to be there, and was not impressed that the neighbours couldn't even be bothered to walk down the length of their garden paths.

By Easter, I was beginning to agree with Madi and had almost resigned myself to the fact that the neighbours and I would never be friends – just neighbours. Almost. But I wasn't quite ready to give up hope, and I've always been an optimist.

And then the miracle of spring happened, and it wasn't just the flowers that burst into life.

One warm May morning, when I was planting flowers in my front garden and I glanced up and spotted Adele watching me from the sitting room of Far Cottage, I smiled and waved and was about to look away when I got the surprise of my life. Adele waved back. Not only that, the woman actually smiled.

As if this was contagious, later that same week, Marcus, who lived in End Cottage, also reciprocated my cheery wave. This time it was me who was looking out of my sitting room window and Marcus was marching up his path towards his front door. For some reason, he glanced towards Middle Cottage, perhaps to admire the new window boxes brimming with fragrant flowers that I had planted, and the pots of varying shapes, sizes and bright colours lining the path to my own front door, and instead of quickly averting his gaze as he usually did, he waved and smiled. It was a quick wave and a brief smile but it filled me with joy and I jumped up and down with delight, and then called Madi to tell her the news.

'I know it's hardly big news,' I had said, 'but I finally feel as if they've accepted me. And maybe, in a couple of years, all three of us might even become friends.'

I was joking of course. I was determined to find out their names by the end of May, and to have held a conversation, however short, with at least one of them, but preferably both, by the end of June.

I had got my wish. The warmer weather had brought both my neighbours out into their gardens and although the fences, bushes and trees in the back gardens were far too tall for any of us to see one another, the hedges dividing the front gardens were only a couple of feet high and I took every opportunity to pop outside and chat if either neighbour ventured out.

By the first week of July, I not only knew my neighbours' names were Adele and Marcus, I had also discovered Adele worked in a bakery and adjoining café in Fairlight Bay, called Fairlight Bakes, and Marcus owned his own business, also in Fairlight Bay. At that stage, I had yet to ascertain what his business was as he hadn't elaborated, but I thought it might involve working outdoors because we had been briefly discussing the weather one morning when it looked as if it was about to pour with rain, and Marcus had said that he hoped it wouldn't as he had a big job on and he'd rather it wasn't rained off.

When I invited them both to a small, summer BBQ in August, I had high hopes of them attending. Sadly, neither had.

'Small steps,' I had said to Madi.

'Why bother?' Madi had replied, she and Tristan having yet again driven hundreds of miles from Somerset for that BBQ – and to spend the Bank Holiday weekend with me. 'I know you think everyone should get on with everyone else and we should all be friends with our neighbours, but some people just like to live their lives on their own terms and keep themselves to themselves.'

I could understand that some people liked their privacy but surely it was better to chat to one's neighbours and at the very least, to pass the time of day with them rather than to ignore them and refuse their hospitality?

I had hoped Adele and Marcus would join me at the Horrible Halloween Hop, the annual dance held in Fairlight Bay on the Saturday night closest to Halloween. I had mentioned it to each of them several times throughout September and October but they had both changed the subject or each said they'd think about it, in a way that made me certain they had no intention of doing any such thing.

'I'm worried they may be lonely,' I told Madi.

'Why? Just because they both appear to live on their own? You live alone, but you're not lonely, are you?'

'No. But I've got friends and my family.'

Madi had tutted. 'And so have they. You told me yourself that you've seen people come and go to both cottages over the months you've lived there. Perhaps their lives are full enough and they don't feel the need to be friends with you. Even though it's their loss because you're so lovely, of course.'

I had laughed at that. 'She adds hastily. Hmm. I know you're probably right and yet ... I don't know why and I can't really explain it but ... they both seem sad somehow. And the weird thing is, they both smile and say hello to me now, and they'll even stop and chat, but they won't smile and say hello to one another and I haven't seen them exchange one word. That's odd, isn't it? They've both lived on Midwinter Lane for years, so they've both told me.'

'Yes,' Madi agreed. 'That is strange. Perhaps they had a row or something. Or perhaps they dated once and didn't hit it off. You said they're around the same age, didn't you?'

'Yes. Although I don't know for sure because I haven't asked their ages and they haven't offered to tell me, but I don't think they're that much older than us. I would say they're both in their early forties. I asked Adele about it a few weeks ago. Not about their ages. About why they don't seem to acknowledge one another. She almost bit my head off. "I don't want to talk about that", was all she would say, and the look she gave me could've turned me to ice.'

'Yep. That definitely sounds as if they've fallen out. You'll have to find out why, won't you?'

'Absolutely,' I had agreed.

'Although the most worrying thing you said was that they're not much older than us,' Madi added. 'How did we get to be thirty-six so quickly?'

'I have no idea. I still feel like twenty-one. Unfortunately, I don't look that age.'

'Tell me about it,' Madi said with a sigh.

By November, nothing much had changed with my neighbours, as I had told Madi when she asked for an update.

'They might've also ignored my invitation to join me for the Big Bonfire Night in Fairlight Bay, but things will be different this Christmas. This Christmas, we'll all be friends at the very least.'

'I admire your optimism,' Madi had said. 'And your staying power. I'd have told them to stuff it by now.'

Madi and I had been neighbours, and that was how we had met when we were both twenty-one. We both rented small studio flats in the same low-rise block in Bromley in Kent – cheaper than living in London but still easily commutable to the City where we both worked, oddly enough, as we had quickly discovered, in high-rise office buildings next door to one another. We soon became friends and over the years we shared highs and lows, heartaches and new loves, career wins and losses, and everything in between.

We were more like sisters than best friends by the time we moved from the tiny studio flats we had rented to a large, two-bedroom flat a short distance along the road, which we had bought together. Like so many others around our age, neither of us could ever have afforded to buy a place on our own. Property in and around London had always been expensive, but together we each managed to get a foot on the first rung of the property ladder.

Madi had worked her way up the corporate ladder to become an executive assistant to a high-flying executive in a leading global technology, consulting and research company.

Two years ago, she had gone on a date with her boss, who subsequently decided he no longer wanted to fly-high in the City but wanted to move down to Somerset and start his own cider-making business instead. He told Madi about his dream, and, as Madi had always wanted to live in the countryside, when Tristan asked her to go with him, she had instantly said yes.

I had worked in the Human Resources department of one of the world's largest international banks and had also worked my way up towards the glass ceiling that still existed in that bank, but before I could break through, technology had taken over. The bank had revamped many of its HR services, making much of it digital, meaning there were fewer jobs for humans. I was assured my position was secure, but when the bank asked for voluntary redundancies, I stepped forward. I had been considering a change for a while and with Madi moving to Somerset, I decided it was time to make my own break from the City to the countryside.

Madi and Tristan had told me that Madi would keep her share in the flat so that I wouldn't need to sell up and move elsewhere, but I had already made up my mind to do so, and the flat was sold and the profits shared equally.

I had chosen to move to Sussex, not Somerset. It was where my family lived. But I must admit, the urge to join Madi in the West Country, and possibly live close to her and Tristan, was strong.

Until my mum suggested that Madi and Tristan might not want their single friend tagging along as they embarked on their new adventure. I believe Mum had said it with the best of intentions, but her words hit home and although I knew Madi would miss me as much as I would miss her, I decided I should give them some space.

It was only later that I realised Mum was slightly hurt by my wanting to move to Somerset to be close to my best friend rather than move back to Sussex to be close to my family.

That was a bit of a surprise. Mum had never shown any great desire for me to live close by, before. I think she was pleased when I moved to London at the age of twenty-one. I had returned to Fairlight Bay for a few weekend visits throughout the year and Mum, as well as Dad and Gran, had always said they had missed me while I was away. Yet as Sunday evening drew near, Mum frequently checked her watch and said she didn't want me to get stuck in traffic, and that I shouldn't leave my departure until late, as most road accidents occurred after dark. I wasn't sure if that was true. I kept meaning to look it up, but I'm not really sure I wanted to know.

On the whole, I'm glad I decided to come home to Fairlight Bay. Gran was getting on in years, and now lived in a home on the outskirts of town, but she went to my parents for Sunday lunch every weekend, so time spent with her was precious.

And I loved living near the sea again. The sea was the main thing I missed when I lived in Bromley. Apart from my family, of course.

I had been able to purchase Middle Cottage on Midwinter Lane outright and still had money to spare. I wasn't sure then what I wanted to do once I had moved but I knew I would want to work, and would need to do so, because at the age of thirty-five, as I was then, retirement – even early retirement – was a long way off.

I also knew I would have to do something I loved. The idea of starting my own business was inspired by Tristan and his cider.

'I want to spend the rest of my working life doing something I love,' he had told me when I'd asked him why he'd chosen that. 'I love apples. I love cider. I love making things and working with my hands. I love the outdoors. And I've loved Somerset since I was a kid. I saw the farm and apple orchards close to where I'd holidayed every year with my parents as a kid, were up for sale and I just knew that was it,' he had explained.

I had hoped I would have a similar epiphany but when I had moved to Middle

Cottage, I still had no idea of what I wanted to do with my life.

Since Madi and I had moved out of the flat we had shared for years and gone our separate ways, so many things had changed. Having been neighbours long before that, we still hadn't adjusted to living so far away from one another. Yet one thing that hadn't changed, was our friendship. We may now be hundreds of miles apart but we texted, phoned or video called each other constantly. Sometimes even when neither of us had anything particular to say. Just like today.

I sipped the coffee I had made and luxuriated in its warmth, my fingers entwined around the mug.

'I'm nipping into town once I've showered and dressed,' I said. 'And I'm having lunch with the family. But I need to wait for the water to heat up first. After that, it's back here to finish putting up the rest of the Christmas decorations outside, which will cheer me up, and the official lighting switch on will be happening as soon as that's done, later today. The two grinches are fine. But they did both give me odd looks when I started putting up my outdoor decorations on Friday. Last year, I couldn't even get a smile out of either of them, let alone a 'Merry Christmas', or any other holiday greeting they might prefer. This Christmas, I'm determined they'll not only exchange cheery festive greetings, they'll put up some decorations and they'll join in the fun.'

'Good luck with that,' Madi said. 'We're putting our decorations up today. If I can summon up the energy to get off the sofa, that is. I'll send you some photos when we're done and you send me some of yours. I wish we could get together this Christmas, but you're still coming down here for New Year, aren't you?'

'Definitely. I'm looking forward to it.'

'But not as much as you're looking forward to Christmas, right?'

I sniggered. 'I can't help it if I love Christmas. And it's just as well I do. If I hadn't, I wouldn't have started my own business selling Christmas decorations.'

That idea had come to me last Christmas after mulling over what Tristan had told me about his own business venture. Luckily for me, not only was he good with his hands, Tristan was a whizz with technology, and he had set up a website for me when I had gone to stay at Apple Orchard Farm for a few days in January.

With Madi's help, the three of us had decided on a name, and Midwinter Cottage Decorations was born. That sounded better than Middle Cottage and I considered changing the name of my own home to

Midwinter Cottage, but that would entail making a request to the local authority and paying a fee, and if they approved my request, notifying the Royal Mail and then my bank, doctor, dentist, etc., so I put that notion to one side.

Tristan, Madi and I had organised some advertising on social media, for my new business, and within a matter of days, orders began to trickle in, picking up pace when I added Valentine decorations at the end of January, and Easter decorations in March.

In April, I had also rented a stall at the Fairlight Bay Market which was held every Thursday throughout the year. People visited from far and wide and word soon spread of my Midwinter Cottage range of gorgeous and often quirky decorations, most of which were handmade either by me, or by people I had met while shopping at various other craft markets and fairs.

I added more seasonal decorations, like summer bunting, autumn wreaths, and spooky items for Halloween, and by the end of November, my business was booming. So much so that I was now thinking of taking on some extra help.

'That's true,' said Madi, as I finished my coffee and walked back to the sink. 'Who would've believed when we first met that both of us would one day leave London for good and be running our own businesses? Well, in my case, jointly running a business with my fiancé.'

'Not me. I thought I'd be head of HR one day. But I'm so glad I'm not. We're both much happier now than we ever were working for others, aren't we?'

'Definitely. But I do wish we lived closer to one another. I miss you so much.'

'Same here,' I said, turning on the tap to rinse out my mug before I put it in the dishwasher. 'Arggh! Oh hell! Now I've soaked myself. This stupid tap thinks it's a shower. One minute it's working fine, the next it's spraying water everywhere.'

Madi laughed. 'Haven't you got that fixed? I thought you had a plumber booked for last week.'

We usually chatted most days but the past week had been hectic for both of us and we'd only spoken briefly once or twice.

'Yeah. So did I. It seemed he thought otherwise. I tried calling him several times after he missed the appointment but all I got was his voicemail. I left polite messages at first, but after the fifth call I sort of lost it and I left him a slightly snarky message. Now I think he's blocked my calls. All I get is a message saying, "The person you're trying to reach is unavailable". I'll have to find another one, but plumbers, it seems, are rarer than

Santa's magic dust.'

'Santa's magic dust?'

'The stuff that makes the reindeer fly.'

'Of course. Silly me. Couldn't the heating engineer you need to fix your boiler, sort out the plumbing too? I know not all plumbers can deal with central heating but I think all central heating engineers can deal with plumbing. Although I may be wrong. Tristan deals with all that.'

'I suppose so. I'll have to do another search online and see what I can find.'

Madi laughed again. 'Or you could ask your neighbours. And you could get them to help with your decorations too. That should get them in the Christmas spirit. I'd better let you go and find your plumber slash heating engineer. Call me later with an update.'

'Will do,' I said, dabbing at my saturated dressing gown with reams of kitchen paper towel. 'I'm already wet, so I might as well go and have my shower. The water should be warming up by now. Give my love to Tristan.'

Two

'Alec Richman Heating and Plumbing. How may I help you?' The voice took me by surprise, partly because a human being, not a machine, had answered, and partly because the man was so polite and friendly, but mainly because I hadn't expected the voice to sound quite as deep and gravelly. Or as ... sexy.

'Oh. Erm. I need someone to come and fix my heating. And my kitchen tap. Would you be able to do that, please?'

'I wouldn't be a particularly good heating engineer and plumber if I couldn't. Where do you live?'

'Middle Cottage. On Midwinter Lane. It's on Midwinter Ridge in the tiny hamlet of Midwinter. Near Fairlight Bay.'

'I know Midwinter Lane.' He sounded amused by my directions, which I'd given because his website stated, "we cover East Sussex", and as that was a rather large area,

27

I had no idea if he would've heard of such a tiny place as Midwinter. Apparently, he had. 'Is it an emergency?'

'Erm. It's December and it's freezing today. So yes, I would say so.'

'Do you have kids?'

'Sorry?'

'Do you have kids?' he repeated.

'N-o.' That was a weird thing to ask.

'Do you live with elderly relatives?'

'No. And before you ask, I don't have a dog, a cat, or a hamster. I live alone. Erm. I need a heating engineer and a plumber, not a date. What has any of that got to do with this?' I kept my voice light and friendly but it crossed my mind that I might've called a weirdo.

His laugh, however, was pleasant. Very pleasant. Almost melodic.

An image of the man developed in my mind's eye. Tall, broad shouldered, athletic build, long legs, a cheerful and sexy smile, dark hair and dark, straight eyebrows framing equally dark eyes, above a full mouth and a firm jaw.

A shiver ran through me, and it wasn't because I was cold. The heating had been on for some time now and the cottage was as toasty as could be. Of course, the man would probably be the complete opposite of what I had imagined. Which was just as well.

Because the image I had conjured up was that of Berry's brother, Paul. And I shouldn't be thinking about Paul in any way, shape, or form. The man had a girlfriend.

Perhaps this Alec Richman would be short, fat and hairy. In fact, I rather hoped he would be, because the last thing I needed in my life was to have a crush on both Berry's brother, and a plumber. Or on anyone for that matter. I had a business to run and Christmas to prepare for, and, unlike Madi's, my love life had always been a bit of a disaster.

Although … it had been a long time since I had had a crush on anyone, prior to meeting Paul. The last date I had been on was before I had moved to Middle Cottage so that was well over a year ago now. Perhaps meeting someone wouldn't be so bad after all. And with Christmas coming, it would be lovely to have someone to snuggle up with in front of a roaring, log fire on the cold, winter nights. Not that I had a roaring log fire to snuggle in front of. Or any fire for that matter.

Alec interrupted my thoughts with a small cough. 'As you said, it's December and it's freezing. I'm trying to establish how much of an emergency it is. My list is longer than Santa's right now, so if you don't have kids or elderly people living in your home, you won't be at the top of my list. Sorry.

What's the problem with the heating?'

'If I knew that, I wouldn't be calling you.' I laughed even though it wasn't funny.

'Fair point. What I meant was, is it the boiler? Or is it a problem with the programmer? Is the pilot light on?'

'Yes. And I managed to turn the heating on manually.'

'So you've got heating then?'

'Yes. But it didn't come on this morning, so it might not come on tomorrow either.'

'But it's working okay other than that?'

'Yes. It seems to be.'

'And you've got hot water?'

'I have now, but it was tepid when I had my shower.'

'Then it's not really an emergency, is it? I'm rushed off my feet as it is. I might be able to squeeze you in on Tuesday morning. Early. If it's not a big job.'

'Tuesday? But ... it's Sunday today.'

'Tell me about it. Sorry. Tuesday's the earliest I can do. You could try someone else.'

I had already called five others. Two just laughed. One simply hung up. The others didn't even answer their phones. But then again, as I had said, it was Sunday today.

'But ... it *is* an emergency. Maybe not to you. And perhaps not as much as some others, but it's an emergency as far as I'm concerned. Your website states that you provide same day emergency call-outs, so why can't you come today? Are you really that busy?'

'As we both agree, it's December and it's freezing,' he repeated. 'This month and next are my busiest times. Tuesday is the earliest I can do.'

'What am I supposed to do until then?'

'You could stay somewhere else. It's only a couple of days. Surely you can manage until then?'

'That's easy for you to say. Your heating is working perfectly, I don't doubt.'

'It is, thanks. Shall I book you in for Tuesday?'

'Do I have a choice?'

'Not if you want me to come and look at it, no.'

I slumped onto the sofa and glanced out of the sitting room window. There was still no sign of the sun even though it had supposedly risen over an hour ago. The sky was as leaden as my current mood and the sight of my neighbour, Marcus, hurrying down his garden path in his thick padded jacket, jeans and boots, his scarf flapping in the wind, and his woollen hat pulled down low over his ears, made me shiver, despite the cottage having finally warmed up. In fact, I was now feeling a little too warm, having dressed in a pair of black twill trousers, a white cotton blouse, and a Christmas-themed red and green jumper.

Marcus was heading towards the wooden footbridge a few metres from our front gates. It was our only means of crossing Midwinter Brook, other than wading through the water. There was an area on the other side of the brook that had reserved parking spaces for our three cottages, the lane itself being far too narrow to allow a vehicle to pass. It was built in the days of horse and carts, and I use the word 'built' somewhat loosely, because even now Midwinter Lane was unadopted and made up of sandstone, rocks, and rubble with the odd smattering of tarmac dotted here and there. The car parking area was a much more recent addition, and thankfully, that had been tarmacked.

I let out a sigh of resignation. 'Then I suppose it'll have to be Tuesday. If that's really the earliest you can do.'

'It is. What's your name?'

'My name's Noelle.'

'Noelle? Well, that's a first. The first Noelle.' He virtually sang the words.

I rolled my eyes. If I had a pound for every time I'd heard that comment over the years, I'd be rich.

'Yes. That's smart, Alec,' I quipped, and then realised it might not be wise to be sarcastic. 'Look. You will turn up, won't you? I'd booked a plumber to fix the tap last week and he never showed. I don't want to wait until Tuesday and then find I need to get someone else.'

'Oh yes. I'd forgotten you mentioned a tap. What's wrong with the tap? Wait. If you knew that you wouldn't need me. Right?' He chuckled. 'What I meant was, is it dripping? Or something else?'

'It thinks it's a shower. But it only does it sometimes. It was fine when I filled the kettle but when I rinsed my mug, I got drenched.'

'Hmm. Sounds like a water pressure problem. I'll sort it out on Tuesday. And I'll be there, Noelle. I promise. If I get a cancellation, or I can make it sooner, I'll let you know.'

'Thanks,' I said. 'I'll see you soon then, I hope.'

I rang off, reluctantly got up from my comfy, navy velvet sofa, and walked to the kitchen, eyeing the tap warily.

Could I refill the kettle without getting drenched? I was yearning for another mug of coffee. I could put on my raincoat, perhaps. At least then if the tap spurted water all over me, I would still be dry.

Or I could go and see my parents earlier than I had planned. Their tap was working perfectly, as far as I knew. I was going there for Sunday lunch in any event. I might as well go early and get a cup of coffee thrown in. If my heating was still playing up later, I would need to ask if I could stay with them until Tuesday, so if I went early, I could build up to asking that. The heating had come on today, but it might not do so later. Or tomorrow. I loved cold weather, frost, ice, and snow, but only when I was dressed for it and was outdoors. Indoors, I expected to be warm and cosy without wearing several layers of jumpers, coats and scarves.

Now I was beginning to wish I had gone for a wood burning stove in my sitting room, or at least kept the old gas fire that was already there. At least then, if my heating gave up, I would still be able to warm at least one room of my cottage. But the thing had looked like a bit of a death trap, so I'd had it taken out. I had meant to get one of those gorgeous, real flame effect electric fires to replace it but for some reason, I still hadn't got around to finding one I liked.

I should've been working instead of considering going to my parents' house early. I needed to make more Christmas decorations; some to fulfil specific online orders, and some to sell at the market in town on Thursday. I had a stall there every Thursday on Market Day, and last week, I sold out. Not one single decoration was left by the time I packed up at five.

Luckily, I had more stock at home, because the Fairlight Bay Christmas Market officially opened on Saturday, and during the festive season, which began in late November in Fairlight Bay, I also had a stall on Saturdays. I'd taken extra stock, just in case, and it was a good thing I had, because yet again, I sold every item.

The market was exceptionally busy on Saturday and all the other stallholders sold out too, meaning everyone was exceedingly happy.

That was why Berry had suggested we should go for that quick drink in The Dog and Duck. The quick drink that had turned into a long and drunken night, and left me with a bit of a hangover this morning.

I had met Berry and her brother, Paul, back in April when, in addition to selling my decorations online, I had also rented a stall at the Fairlight Bay Market.

I had never done anything like that before, having spent most of my working life in an office and then later, having run my fledgeling business of Midwinter Cottage Decorations, from my kitchen table, via my laptop.

So manning a stall in a public market was a somewhat daunting experience, and to help ease me in to being a market stall trader,

Madi had come and spent a few days with me, leaving Tristan at home in Somerset to continue running their own business.

To repay that favour, I had gone to Somerset to stay at Apple Orchard Farm for two weeks in September to help with the apple harvest. I don't recall too much about those two weeks, to be honest, apart from the fact that it was wonderful to spend so much time with Madi again, but I do remember that the cider we drank was delicious. My drink of choice is wine, but I must confess that I drank rather a lot of cider during those two weeks.

Well, someone had to sample the goods, didn't they?

Actually, I didn't, because the cider we drank then was cider that had been pressed by the former owner and sold with the property.

I wouldn't be able to sample Tristan and Madi's Apple Orchard Farm Cider until this New Year when the cider made from the apples I helped pick in September would just about be ready to drink.

Tristan assured me that their Apple Orchard Farm Cider would be even better as he had been working on recipes and had tweaked it from the original one. I would get to taste some when I went to stay with them at New Year, and I was already looking forward to it.

Madi, of course, had also never worked on a market stall, so on that first Thursday in April, we were both completely out of our depths. Berry had the stall next to mine and was selling handmade soaps, bath products, and lotions made from all natural ingredients. Some of her soaps were shaped like fruits such as strawberries, apples, and pears, and they all looked good enough to eat. Although I didn't try to. However natural and mainly organic they might have been, soap was still soap as far as I was concerned.

But luckily for me, and for Madi on that first day, Berry took pity on us and showed us the ropes. She taught me how to encourage shoppers to stop at my stall. What to say to them if they were dithering about a purchase. How to seal the deal, and how to ensure I obtained either an email address or a contact number, so that I could send them offers and news of new products.

When her brother Paul arrived to help her pack up, and to give her a lift home because her own car had broken down, they also showed us The Dog and Duck pub which I had never been to before. It was hidden behind Market Square and approached via a twitten, or a cat creep as they are also called in Fairlight Bay. Basically that's a narrow passageway between two buildings, often, but not always, with steps. The twitten leading from Market Square to The Dog and Duck pub was narrow and dark because the upper storeys of the old buildings overhung the passageway. The ground floors housed an art and craft shop on one side, and an antiques store on the other. The twitten led out into another, smaller square with the pub, a former stable, and more antique shops fronting the square. I thought I knew all the hidden gems in town, but I must've missed this one.

That was the first drunken night of many. Berry certainly liked a drink. Paul hardly drank at all and was, and has been ever since, the designated driver. Which was why I had assumed that it was he who brought me home last night.

Having now decided an earlier visit to my parents was the best option today, I would need to rethink the rest of my day.

I always had my decorations up, on or around the first of December. Even when I moved last year, they were up, inside and out by the second. Although I did have help from the removal team last year. But this year, I had been so busy running my business that I hadn't even thought about my own decorations until Friday, when I got them down from the loft.

I started with the outdoor decorations,

placing my Christmas silhouettes of a snowman, a deer, and a singing penguin, on the front lawn. I positioned my candy cane path lights either side of my path, hung my handmade wreath on the front door, and fixed my boughs of holly and pine, entwined with Christmas lights, around the door frame and along the downstairs window sills. I also managed to trim the upstairs window sills to match those downstairs, but to hang the rest of the lights, I needed a ladder. I had one in the garden shed but by the time I'd done everything else it was getting dark and I wasn't climbing a ladder on my own in the dark, in case I fell off.

There wasn't that much left to do as far as the outdoor decorations were concerned, but as I was at the Christmas Market all day yesterday, I had planned to finish the outside lights today. The problem with the heating had thrown my schedule off balance though.

My original plan had been to get up early, make the Christmas decorations I needed for my business, and then get the ladder from the shed and finish hanging the lights on the cottage, and decorating the evergreen conifer tree that was growing in the centre of one side of my front lawn, with lights and outdoor baubles. That would have to wait until the afternoon, when I got back from my parents' house.

There was a lot to do inside, so my decorations would be late this year. Especially as I also needed to get some Christmas decorations made for my business. If I started those now, I wouldn't want to stop, and I couldn't be late for Sunday lunch. Mum would never forgive me. No. Going to their house early, having my longed for second mug of coffee, and asking if I could stay if needed, was my best option now.

I turned off the heating, hoping it would come back on when I returned, threw on my coat, hat, scarf, gloves, and boots, and opened the front door.

A blast of arctic air hit me full in the face and took my breath away for a moment. It was colder than I had thought and the wind was bitter this morning. There was no way I was putting outdoor decorations up in this, unless the weather changed this afternoon.

Perhaps I should've left the heating on. Knowing my luck, the pipes would freeze up, burst, and flood the cottage.

'What is wrong with you, Noelle?' I chastised myself. I was usually an optimist and looked on the bright side no matter what, not a pessimist who decided that everything would be a disaster even when it wasn't.

Perhaps it was my hangover.

And on that subject, I reminded myself to phone Berry and ask who had brought me home last night. But more importantly, whether I was still fully clothed when whomever it was, had left.

Three

'Perhaps your father could take a look?' Mum said when I told her about the problem with my heating, and my faulty tap.

I'm not sure if she was questioning herself, Dad's DIY skills, or my desperation, but knowing that Dad was about as handy as me when it came to DIY, I thought she was joking – and laughed.

Dad, who had already quirked a brow but had pretended not to hear Mum's comment and had continued to read the Sunday papers, shot me a look, and grinned. We both knew there was no way he was going to take a look at my heating problem.

'If the boiler's still playing up and the heating doesn't come on again this afternoon, may I come and stay here the night, please? I hate waking up in a freezing cold room. I can leave the heating on all day if I must. Although that would mean paying a fortune in my bills. But I can't sleep if the heating's on all night.'

'You're lucky to have heating,' Gran said. 'When I was a girl we had one fire to heat the whole house. And we had an outside loo.'

Mum rolled her eyes. 'No you didn't, Mother. That was your mother, not you. You grew up in a house with central heating and a bathroom. And your parents had an ensuite.'

'Fiddlesticks,' said Gran. 'You weren't born so you don't know. Times were hard until I met Harold. He was the one who bought my parents a new house with all the mod-cons.'

Gran lived in a home for the elderly on the outskirts of Fairlight Bay, but she'd come round for Sunday lunch as always and was sitting in an armchair opposite Dad, knitting something that I was fairly sure would end up in my Christmas stocking.

Gran was good at knitting, even if her memory wasn't what it once was, her fingers were as agile as ever, but the three balls of wool jiggling on the carpet as her needles clicked and clacked and wove the strands of wool together were, it had to be said, colours I wouldn't be seen dead in.

One was vomit-green, one was vivid orange, so bright it seared my eyes just looking at it, and the third one was ... I wasn't sure there was a word to describe it.

Although I suppose it must've been called something otherwise how would one be able to order more of it, if required?

Or perhaps the question should've been, why would anyone want to order any of it in the first place? Puce would be the closest, I supposed, but it reminded me of dog poo, to be honest.

Perhaps I'd be lucky, and Gran was knitting whatever it was for Mum, not me. Or possibly for Dad.

'Just one night?' Mum asked, looking anxious.

'Two at the most,' I said, trying not to feel unwanted. 'The plumber guy has promised he'll be there on Tuesday.'

Mum brightened. 'Then of course you can stay, dear. He's sure he'll be able to mend it?'

'Until we know what's wrong, I can't really say. But he sounded confident.'

He also sounded gorgeous, but Mum didn't need to know that.

Mum and I had a fairly good relationship, but we weren't best friends or anything, like some daughters and mothers say they are.

Mind you, I wouldn't have told my mum the stuff I told Madi and Berry even if we were friends. Mum was ... old fashioned in many ways.

When I asked if she had some headache tablets, I didn't tell her it was because I had a hangover from drinking far too much in The Dog and Duck the previous night. I told her it was from the stress and worry of waking up in a freezing cold cottage and knowing there was a problem with my heating.

I rarely got headaches, and I was usually as fit as a fiddle, as Gran would say, so I didn't have any headache tablets at the cottage. Maybe I should get some in, just in case.

'How's your little *business* going?' Mum asked during lunch, emphasising the word business in a way that made it sound as if it wasn't a business at all.

She called it my little hobby for several months, but when I told her and Dad last month how much money I was making, she finally agreed to take it a bit more seriously.

'It's going great,' I said, not bothering to elaborate.

I knew she wasn't really interested. Mum had never worked a day in her life. Unless you call bringing up a child, work.

Which come to think of it, Mum did.

'You were *such* hard work as a child,' she often said, once again putting the emphasis on one word to really rub it in.

She loved me, I was certain of that, but she had wanted a son, not a daughter, and as

I was an only child, Mum never seemed to get over the disappointment, and as strange as it might seem, she wasn't really equipped to deal with a daughter.

It had been Gran who had plaited my hair. Gran who had taught me how to sew and knit and bake. Gran who had picked out party dresses, and bows, and sparkly shoes, even if it had been Mum, or more accurately, Dad, who had insisted on paying for most of them.

Gran had enrolled me in ballet classes, the brownies, and swimming lessons. But Gran had also signed me up for karate, and the running club, believing that every girl should be able to look after herself if the need arose, and if she couldn't, she should be able to run fast enough to get out of danger.

I'm not sure why Gran also arranged for me to have piano lessons, horse riding lessons, and to join the local astronomy club, but I think that was the dreamer in her.

She loved music and she adored horses, but her own mum hadn't been able to afford such things, and neither had Gran when she was first married.

As for the astronomy club, well, Gran had always maintained that there was no way we were alone in this wonderful, amazing Universe, so perhaps she hoped I might be able to spot a spaceship or something.

It was Gran's second husband, Harold, who had money, and marrying him, after her first husband passed away, meant that Gran could give up her job in the local department store, and that Mum could have almost anything she wanted. Within reason. And as Gran had said, Harold paid for a new house for Gran's own parents.

Mum was just a few months old when her biological dad died, and three years-old when Gran remarried, so Mum remembered her own childhood as idyllic, having little or no memory of the years when Gran had struggled financially.

Gran told me that the first thing she bought after her second marriage, was a telescope. Harold bought her a piano, followed soon after by a horse.

Mum hated her own piano lessons, was allergic to horses, and the only time she ever looked up was to check if it looked like it might rain. Unlike my hair, which was long and straight and light brown, Mum's was shoulder-length, blonde, and curled like a corkscrew when it got wet. Which was probably why she also hated swimming.

Thanks to her stepdad's wealth, Mum didn't need to work to support herself through university, and as she met Dad on the first day there, and they married two days after they both graduated, she didn't work once she was a wife. Other than bringing me up, of course. Which, as I have said, was apparently *such* hard work.

Four

After lunch, I phoned Berry.

'I had a hangover this morning,' I said stopping to sit on the cold, hard, plastic seat at the bus stop shelter. 'I've still got a bit of a headache, even though I took some tablets a while ago.'

'Been to lunch with the folks?' she asked.

'Uh-huh. Erm. Did Paul give me a lift home last night?'

'Can't you remember?' I could hear the laughter in her voice.

'Not exactly, no.'

'Of course he gave you a lift. You could hardly walk.' Now she laughed aloud.

'Erm. Did you come with him?'

'Why? What's up?'

'I don't remember getting changed into my PJs, that's all. I wondered if either you ... or he ... helped me.'

Now she roared with laughter.

'It was me, you silly cow. Do you

honestly think I'd let my brother undress you? He did carry you up the stairs though. I was going to stay the night because you were really out of it. But you insisted you were fine and after I got you into your PJs and made you clean your teeth, you did seem to sober up, so I thought you were okay. Fancy a hair of the dog?'

'I do, actually. But I can't. I've got Christmas decorations to make. Plus, I want to put up the rest of my own decorations. The outside ones at least. I haven't even started on the indoors yet. My heating's playing up and I may need to spend a night or two at my parents, so I've got to get home now and get as much done as I can. When I'm at my place I can work till late and get up early, but Mum doesn't like me making decorations at their house. She says I make such a mess and she finds glitter for weeks afterwards. They bolt the front door on the dot of ten, so I need to be there by nine-fifty-five at the latest. It's almost three now so that only gives me a few hours.'

'I've said it before and I'll say it again. Your mum is weird. But what's this about your heating? Have you called out an engineer?'

'Yep. He can't come till Tuesday. Apparently, it's only an emergency if you've got kids or old people in your home. People in their thirties can freeze. I do have heating. At least I did this morning. But I have to turn it on and off manually.'

'Heaven forbid!'

'Sarcasm is not appropriate. How would you like waking up in a freezing bedroom and having to go downstairs to turn on the heating, and then wait hours for the place to warm up?'

'Okay. You're right. I wouldn't like that. You could come and stay with me. But you'd have to share my bed, and my sitting room and kitchen are tiny, as you know, so I'm not sure how helpful that would be.'

'Thanks for the offer, but I'll go home and work. I'm not driving today because I'm not sure I'm fit to do so, and if the police stopped me, I'm fairly certain I'd still be over the limit. It's downhill to Mum and Dad's but it's all uphill going home, so that also takes time.'

'How did you get to your parents' house?'

'I walked.'

'In this weather! It's freezing.'

'I know. I've stopped at the bus shelter near Mum and Dad's but I don't think many buses run on a Sunday. I was going to ask Dad for a lift but then they'd ask why I wasn't driving.'

'You're thirty-six, Noelle. You're allowed

to get drunk.'

'Yeah? You tell my parents that.'

'Wait there. I'll get Paul to come and get you and give you a lift. I would do it myself but I'm probably still over the limit too.'

'No! You can't ask Paul to drop everything to take me home. Isn't he with his girlfriend?'

'Blimey. You were drunk last night, weren't you? Didn't you hear the blazing row they had just before the pub closed? Well the blazing row she had. Paul just took it in his stride as he always does. But she walked out and said she never wanted to see him again.'

'What?' I almost slid off the seat in the bus stop shelter. 'How did I miss that?'

'I think you might've fallen asleep by then. Anyway, it's over.'

'It's over? Really? Just like that?'

'Paul says it's been a long time coming. And let's be honest, neither you or I like her, do we? She was always telling him to do this or do that or do something else. But I can tell you all about it later. Let me call him first and tell him to come and pick you up.' The irony of that statement wasn't lost on me. 'Are you sure you don't have time for a quick drink?'

'Well. Maybe just the one. And I do mean, one, Berry.'

'Great. I'll call Paul now and we'll see you in a mo.'

Paul and his girlfriend had broken up? Could this really be true? I had to tell Madi right away.

'You're kidding?' she said when I shared the news. 'See. I told you things could only get better today, didn't I?'

I laughed at that. 'I'm not sure how Paul and his girlfriend splitting up makes things better.'

'Of course it does. It means the hunk of a man is free and single. Now's your chance. Wouldn't you like to have a man in your life?'

'Erm. Yes. It would be nice. And I'd definitely like to have Paul in my bed, I can't deny that. But I'm so busy with my business that I'm not sure I have time to start a relationship, as tempting as it is. Besides, just because they've split up, it doesn't mean he'd ask me out. I know he likes me as a friend, but I have no idea if he'd consider me as his girlfriend.'

'There's only one way to find out. Show the guy you're interested, and see where it goes from there. And there's no time like the present.'

I had also told her that Berry was getting him to come and pick me up and that we were going to the pub for a quick drink.

'I don't know, Madi.' I was already having doubts, despite the fact that I had had similar thoughts the moment Berry had told me. 'What if we did start dating, and we slept together, and then discovered we didn't get on, or something? That would make things difficult between us, and it would threaten my friendship with Berry. I'm not sure it's worth the risk.'

'Worth the risk? What is wrong with you today? Why are you looking on the dark side of this? You're usually an optimist, not a pessimist. What if things worked out so well between you two that you got married and had kids? Then you'd have a new family. A loving family. I'm not saying you don't have a loving family now, but yours isn't the touchy-feely sort, is it? Apart from you and your Gran. Paul, Berry, and their parents, are definitely more affectionate, aren't they? Isn't that what you want? Isn't that what you've always wanted?'

Madi knew me so well. Possibly better than I knew myself.

'Yes,' I admitted. 'I've always wanted that. And you're right. Things might go well between us. Assuming he is interested in me. And there's no harm in finding out. I'm not sure why I'm not my usual, cheery self. Especially as it's now December and so close to Christmas.' I let out a long sigh.

'I think it's those neighbours of yours,' Madi said. 'You had such high hopes of the three of you becoming friends, and yet here you are, one year later, not that much closer to being friends than you were the day you moved in.'

'That's not strictly true. We talk now.'

But Madi was right. I had initially had high hopes for the three of us becoming friends, and the two of them keeping me at arm's length had made me feel ... well, a bit like Mum always made me feel. That I wasn't quite good enough.

That was why I had always made myself look on the bright side of life. I wanted to be open-minded and open-hearted. I wanted to see the best in people. I wanted to love ... and to be loved.

It wasn't simply that though. Since Adele and Marcus had finally started speaking to me, and I was getting to know them, I had discovered that the two of them had a lot of things in common.

They had both told me in conversation, and without either of them realising I was asking specific questions, that they liked long walks, especially in Fairlight Glen. They both loved wildlife, and birdwatching. They both loved sailing, yet neither owned a boat, or were even members of the Fairlight Bay sailing club – which was odd. They both liked the same types of food, and films, and so many other little things that it made me wonder if Madi had been right and they had once dated or something.

But if so, why hadn't that worked out? And why did they ignore one another, even though they now spoke to me?

I really needed to get to the bottom of this and I needed to speed things up. I might be utterly and completely wrong, but something inside me told me that Adele and Marcus were made for one another. I just had to find a why to get them both to see what I saw. Or, if they had once dated and something had gone wrong, to find a way to put that right.

Maybe Madi was also right about Paul. And as his car turned into the road and he headed towards me, I smiled.

'Paul's here,' I told Madi. 'I'll call you later.'

'Make sure you do,' she said. 'And I want to hear all the naughty little details, if there are any. Which I sincerely hope there will be.'

'Your chariot has arrived,' Paul said with a gorgeous smile, after pulling up at the bus stop and opening his front window.

'Thanks for this,' I said, getting into the passenger seat while having a few naughty thoughts of my own. 'No Berry?'

'I thought I'd pick you up first, as you were waiting in the cold. She's in the warm so we'll get her now.' He headed towards her flat. 'And talking of cold, Berry said you've got problems with your heating.'

'I have,' I said, thinking that Paul could keep me warm if I played my cards right. 'I've booked someone to sort it out, hopefully, but he can't come until Tuesday.'

'Tuesday? Well, I suppose December's a busy month for plumbers. Heating breakdowns, burst pipes, and all that. Are you staying with your parents until it's fixed?'

'Yes. Much to Mum's delight.'

Our eyes met and he smiled as if he could read my mind. Which maybe he could.

'If that gets too much, there's a spare room at my place.'

I almost choked. Had he just offered me his spare bedroom?

'Oh! Erm. Thanks. That ... that's so kind.'

And oh, so tempting. Was it too late for me to say Mum said it wasn't convenient for me to stay at their house?

'And I have heating,' he added with a wink.

Who needed heating when a gorgeous guy like Paul winked and smiled and made all the blood in my veins boil with pure lust and set all my senses on fire?

'When can I move in?'

He looked at me again as we stopped at a set of traffic lights and I was sure steam must be coming out of my ears. Dear god, this man was *soooo* sexy.

'Whenever you like,' he replied his words dripping with honey.

Oh.

My.

God!

Was Paul saying what I thought he was saying?

The loud ring of his phone broke the spell ... and the sexual tension. Which was just as well because if it hadn't, I might've thrown myself onto his lap and had sex with him right then and there. Even if the traffic lights turned green.

But the name that flashed up on his dashboard display dampened my enthusiasm. It was his girlfriend. Or ex-girlfriend.

He hesitated for a moment and then rejected the call, throwing me an embarrassed and boyish sort of smile.

'Nothing to say,' he said, and then cleared his throat as the lights did change to green and he concentrated on turning right and avoiding the cyclist who didn't seem sure where his bike should be.

'Berry told me about last night,' I said, when the cyclist was out of Paul's way. 'I'm sorry I was so drunk. And thank you for carrying me upstairs.'

He gave me another of those gorgeous

smiles. 'Anytime. I think you slept through the drama. But Berry's filled you in today?'

'Uh-huh. I'm sorry things went wrong between you.'

'Are you?' His eyes briefly scanned my face. 'It's been a long time coming. I should've ended it when...' He gave another small cough. 'A while ago. But I didn't.'

'Not something that can be sorted out?'

'No.' He laughed sardonically. 'Absolutely not. It's over.'

'Wow!' I said, perhaps a little too enthusiastically. 'And you're okay?'

He shot me another look. 'I'm good. You?'

'Me?' What was he asking me now? 'I'm good.'

He smiled and his hands tightened on the wheel. 'Yes you are,' he said, his voice so soft I could hardly hear it.

Five

'What happened next?'

Madi was almost screaming with excitement when I called to tell her about my conversation with Paul. I was back home in Middle Cottage and thankfully, the heating had come on as soon as Paul had flicked the switch.

Yes. Paul had come inside and turned my heating on. And not only my heating. Needless to say, I was more than a little turned on myself.

'Berry got in and we went to the pub. Paul sat next to me and I swear to you, the looks he gave me spoke volumes. Berry seemed oblivious and even when Paul said he'd give me a lift home, she came with us.'

'Why didn't you say something to her?' Madi asked, sounding more irritated than I'd been.

'How could I? She doesn't know I've had the hots for her brother since the first day we met. He had a girlfriend so I've never told Berry I liked him. Well, not in *that* way. She knows I like him as a friend, and she seems happy with that. I'm not sure how she might feel if I tell her I'd like to ... explore the possibilities of a relationship with Paul.'

'Explore that hot and hunky body, you mean.'

'Oh god, yes. Y-e-s!' I coughed to clear my throat. 'Anyway, it was good that Berry came with us. She suggested they could help with the decorations. So now all the outdoor decorations are up and even most of the indoor decorations are done. It's just the Christmas tree for the sitting room that I need to buy and decorate. And the one in my bedroom. The one in the kitchen is done.'

'Did you ask Paul to come back and help with the one in the bedroom?' Madi asked, breathlessly. 'Please say yes. Or is that what you said to Paul?' She laughed at her own joke.

'No. But perhaps I might. I think he does like me. As more than a friend, I mean. So maybe he'll be the one to broach the subject with Berry so that I won't have to.'

'Do you think she'd mind if you two dated? I'd be thrilled if I had a brother and you became an item. Even more so if you married him. Then we'd really be sisters. Well, sisters in law.'

'We're sisters in our hearts,' I said. 'Which is far more important. As for Berry, I honestly don't know. She's never suggested it. But then he wasn't free until now, so why would she? We'll have to see what happens.'

'So how were things left? Did he ask you out? Did he say when you'll see him again.'

I shook my head even though it wasn't a video call.

'No. He just said, 'I'll see you soon, Noelle.' But there was something in the way he said it that made my knees turn to jelly and my body tingle with delight. I'll be seeing Berry on Thursday, at the market, so I might see Paul then. But I'm hoping he'll pop round before then. Or call. Or ... or anything, really. I think I'll be on edge every time the phone rings from now on. In a good way, I mean.'

'Couldn't you have thought of a reason to get him to stay?'

'Not really. I'd said a couple of times in the pub that I should be at home making Christmas decorations for my business, so once we'd finished decorating the cottage, Berry said they should leave me to get on with my business stuff, and that she needed to make more products for her business too. I know Paul helps her with some of that, so they left.'

'Well that's disappointing. So close and yet so far. At least you've got heating.'

'For now, yes. But it didn't come on at the set time, so that does mean I'll have to go and stay with my parents because the timer won't work tomorrow either. Oh, and you'll never guess what. They've forecast snow for Sussex this week.'

'Snow! How fantastic. They've forecast rain for here. Wait. Why aren't you cheering?'

'No heating, remember? Got to stay with my parents, ring any bells?'

'Ah, yes. You love snow, but only if it comes at the right time and when you're cosy and comfy in your own home.'

'Not entirely true. I'd love snow when I come and stay with you and Tristan at the New Year. Basically, I'd love snow anytime, anywhere, other than this week, and apart from when I'm with Mum and Dad. All they do is moan about it. One snowflake and they're off.'

'Are you sure you're not adopted?' Madi laughed.

'Sadly, yes. Mum wouldn't have selected me by choice. Anyway. I must get on and make some Christmas decorations. Curfew at the parents' house is at ten p.m. sharp, and it's almost six now.'

Six

'Where's your car?' Dad asked me the following morning at breakfast.

'Hopefully, where I left it,' I said, having slept far better than I'd expected and feeling decidedly more upbeat and light-hearted today. That might have had something to do with a certain man.

'Which is?' One brow was raised as Dad's knife hovered over his slice of toast.

'At home.'

'What's it doing there?' Mum queried, as if I'd said it was on Mars.

'Again hopefully, nothing it shouldn't be. I expressly told it not to have a party while I was gone.'

Two pairs of eyes stared at me blankly.

'That was a joke,' I said.

'Was it?' said Mum, translated to mean, no it wasn't.

'I left it there because ... I met Berry and Paul for a drink yesterday afternoon, and you know how hot the police are on drink-driving at this time of year. No point in taking any chances.'

'You went for a drink in a pub on a Sunday afternoon?' Mum looked horrified. Dad quirked a brow.

I might as well have committed a human sacrifice, or killed all of Santa's reindeer. Not that Mum would've cared about the reindeer. Or the human sacrifice, probably. But drinking on a Sunday – and in a public bar of all places was beyond the pale.

'I did. Then they came and helped me put up the rest of my Christmas decorations. And I must say, I think the cottage is even more festive than last year.'

Mum gasped. 'You've ... you've done that *again*?'

Sometimes I wonder if my mum knows me at all.

I know for certain that I wasn't adopted, because as I told Madi, Mum wouldn't have chosen me, she'd have chosen a boy, but the older I became the more I sometimes wondered if there was a chance I had been switched at birth, and Mum had got me by mistake.

Except, I looked a little like my dad, and also a lot like Gran had when she was my age. I'd seen many photos of Gran in her thirties and the resemblance was uncanny. The plain truth was, I was more like Gran than Mum.

And oddly enough, Gran occasionally said that Mum was nothing like her.

Perhaps it was Mum who was switched at birth.

I'd never say that though. Not even as a joke. Mum didn't have a sense of humour.

'I have,' I said. 'I'm hoping to get Adele and Marcus to decorate their cottages this year too. Won't that be wonderful? You'll be able to stand on your doorstep, look up at Midwinter Ridge and say to everyone in this street, 'My daughter lives there and she persuaded her neighbours to make their homes look as cheerful and as festive as hers.' Wouldn't that make you feel proud?'

Mum blinked several times and I knew she must be in shock because honey was dripping from her toast onto the tablecloth, and dropping food on the tablecloth was as heinous a crime as drinking in a pub on a Sunday afternoon.

'Don't tease your mother,' Dad said. 'Shall I give you a lift home?'

'That would be great, Dad. Thanks.'

'Any chance you could get that plumber to come sooner?' Dad asked as we headed out of the house.

'If only,' I said. 'But 'tis the season, so you never know. Miracles do happen, they say.'

It was so nice to feel so loved and wanted.

They tried their best, I knew that, and so did I, but sometimes, people just clashed. We'd never had blazing rows, or shouting matches, or huge fall-outs, or anything like that but we were very different people. We all loved each other in our own ways, but we had never understood one another.

What's that old saying? "You can't choose family, but you can choose friends and they can become family", or something like that.

Perhaps I should've moved to Somerset when I had the chance. It might've been better for everyone.

Now there I was again, looking on the dark side. This had got to stop.

If I had moved to Somerset, I wouldn't have met Berry, and I wouldn't have met Paul. I probably would've still started my own business, and maybe I'd have met someone else, but perhaps this was meant to be.

I was fairly certain, having dreamt about Paul all night and gone over and over the things he'd said and the looks he'd given me, that he was going to ask me out. Who knew where things might go from there? My life might be about to turn out even better than I could've hoped.

And if I hadn't moved into Middle Cottage, would whoever had lived there instead been so keen to get Adele and Marcus talking? Would they have wanted to play matchmaker?

This was definitely meant to be.

As the old saying goes, "Everything happens for a reason."

I must stay positive, no matter what.

But if everything happens for a reason, why was my boiler playing up?

Maybe I should cut back on quoting old sayings.

And maybe, like Midwinter Brook, I should simply go with the flow, and wait and see what happened next.

Seven

At least the sun was shining, and after Dad dropped me off, I strolled over the old wooden bridge from the car parking area towards my cottage, looking down at the babbling brook as I did so.

The water looked icy, but it sparkled in the sunshine as it tumbled over the rocks, and playfully tugged at the reeds nestled at its edges. A moorhen glided beneath the bridge and popped out the other side glancing back at me as though it were playing hide and seek. I couldn't help but smile.

I looked up at the clear, blue sky and closed my eyes and listened. All I could hear was the gurgling water, and birdsong. I recognised the robin's melody, and when I opened my eyes, one was perched on top of the red post box situated by the fence of Far Cottage. As I stood and watched it, Adele opened the front door and, on seeing me, briefly raised her hand in a hello gesture.

The robin flew off, but I quickly waved back and shouted, 'Isn't it a beautiful morning?'

I saw the shrug and the hesitation and hurried towards her before she had a chance to step back inside.

'How are you?' I asked, opening her front gate and marching down her garden path. 'I haven't seen you for a few days.'

The expression on her face was one of concern. And anxiety.

'I've been unwell,' she said, avoiding my eyes.

'Oh no. I'm sorry to hear that. Are you feeling better now? Is there anything you need?'

She seemed surprised now. 'Erm. No. I don't need anything ... Thank you. And yes. I'm better now, I think.'

'Let me give you my number,' I said. 'Then, if you're ever ill again, you can text me and I can pick up anything you want or need.'

I'd previously suggested to both Adele and Marcus on separate occasions, that we should exchange numbers, just for emergencies, but each had said there was no need as we lived next door to one another. Which basically meant that neither of them wanted me to have their number.

'Okay,' Adele now said, which I must confess, took me completely by surprise.

So you can imagine my astonishment when she added, 'My phone's in the kitchen. I was about to make some coffee. Would you like a cup? Unless you're too busy, of course. Which you probably are.'

I almost fainted on the spot, and strangely enough, Adele seemed as surprised as I was by her invitation.

'I'd love a cup!' I exclaimed hastily and loudly, before she had a chance to retract. And then in a more reasonable tone I joked, 'I'm never too busy for coffee.'

'Oh. Erm. Come in then,' she said, stepping aside to allow me to pass.

This was the first time I had been inside Far Cottage and although it appeared to be, from what I could see so far as I followed her towards the kitchen, the same layout as mine, the sitting room looked bigger. The door was wide open and there was an old gas fire, like the one I'd had removed, set on a fireplace from the 1930s, a coffee table, a sofa that had seen better days many years ago by the look of it, and a TV on another coffee table pushed into one corner. I hate to say this, but welcoming, it wasn't.

Neither was the dining room opposite. That had a table and a couple of chairs, and that was it. And the cottage was almost as cold as mine was with my heating off. There were radiators but they clearly weren't on.

'Don't tell me your boiler is playing up as well?' I said as she opened the door leading to the kitchen.

She gave me a sheepish look and shook her head as a wave of warm, and deliciously scented air washed over me. She held the door open and closed it behind us once we were both inside.

'No,' she said. 'It's fine. I don't have the heating on when I'm spending most of the day in the kitchen. There doesn't seem much point in heating the entire house when I'm only in one room. Is ... is there a problem with your boiler?'

'Yes. It's not working properly. I woke up to a freezing cold cottage yesterday and I spent last night at my parent's house. There's nothing worse than waking up in a bitterly cold bedroom, is there?'

She stiffened at my comment. 'I prefer a cold bedroom,' she said, but her tone told me that wasn't entirely true.

The kitchen was more modern than the other two rooms, although I had only glanced at those. The huge Aga, however, was ancient, although clearly working much better than my boiler because the kitchen was as warm as toast.

'How do you take your coffee?' She pointed to a pine chair with a padded seat cushion, at a small circular, pine table.

'Milk, no sugar, please.'

'It's only instant. I hope that's okay.'

I sat down and glanced around the room. This was much cosier and a lot more welcoming. The kitchen was clearly the heart of this cottage.

'That's perfect, thanks. What is that heavenly smell?'

She turned and looked at me as if she wasn't certain whether I was being sarcastic or genuine.

'Cinnamon biscuits,' she said a crease forming between her dark brows. 'Erm. Would you like one? I've got a batch cooling, and another one in the oven.'

'Oh yes, please. I adore cinnamon biscuits.'

'Me too,' she smiled.

She switched the kettle on and then picked up a pair of tongs from the counter and lifted a biscuit from the metal cooling rack beside the kettle, and transferred it to a plate. Then she added another, and another, and another.

I hoped they weren't all for me. As much as I loved cinnamon biscuits, I had recently had a Full English breakfast. Mum believed every day should start with a Full English.

Adele placed the plate in the centre of the table and smiled again.

'Help yourself.'

I took a bite and couldn't believe it.

'Oh my god, Adele!' I exclaimed after I swallowed. 'I've never tasted anything as delicious as this. I thought my own Christmas cookies were good but this makes mine pale into second place.'

The surprise on her face was genuine. And then she beamed at me.

'Really? You ... you're not just saying that?'

'Really,' I confirmed. 'These are unbelievably good. I know you said you worked in a bakery and café but I didn't realise you did the baking.'

'I don't. I'm a waitress.'

'A waitress? With baking skills like this? Do you make other things? Or are these your speciality?'

She shrugged. 'I make lots of things. I love baking. It makes me happy.' She smoothed down her apron with both hands and breathed in, pulling in her tummy just a fraction. 'So does eating what I make. As you can no doubt see from the size of me.'

'Size of you? There's nothing wrong with the size of you.'

Adele shook her head crossly. 'Look at me!' She held her arms out at her sides and did a fast twirl. 'I'm overweight, underpaid, and struggling to pay my bills. So what do I do? I spend money on ingredients I can't afford and bake biscuits and cakes and then sit here alone and stuff my face!' She blinked several times and then stared at me open-mouthed, no doubt mirroring my own expression. 'I ... I don't know where that came from,' she continued. 'Ignore me. I ... I didn't mean to say that. This was a bad idea.'

'No, Adele.' I got to my feet and reached out for her hands, taking them in mine and giving them a friendly squeeze, and then, as a tear trickled down her cheek, I pulled her in for a big, and hopefully comforting hug as I wrapped my arms around her. 'This was a good idea. A very good idea. We all have times in our lives when we feel overwhelmed. You've been ill. You're not at your best. It's good to let it all out. I do it all the time with my best friend, Madi. I know you've got friends and probably family too, but I'd like to be your friend, Adele. If you want to be mine, that is.'

She looked me directly in the eye and wiped her own with the back of her hand.

'Really? You ... you mean that? You ... you'd like us to be friends?'

'Absolutely.'

I relaxed my hold on her and she eased herself away to grab a tissue. She blew her nose loudly.

'Still want to be my friend?' she quipped.

I nodded. 'Yes. But I want you to tell me

why that surprises you.'

The kettle clicked itself off and she turned to look at it. 'I'll make the coffee and then I'll tell you.'

I sat down again and waited until she had put two mugs of coffee on the table and we'd both eaten one biscuit.

'Of course,' I said, 'it was these biscuits that sealed the deal. That was a joke, in case you think that might be true. They are delicious, but I've been trying to be a friend since the day I moved in.'

She smiled wanly and let out a long sigh. 'I know you have. At least, I thought you were. But I wasn't sure, you see. And after what happened before. Well. I thought it might be best not to get involved.'

'What happened before? Sorry. I'm not following.'

She shook her head. 'I've seen you chatting with Marcus.'

'I've been trying to be friends with him too. Is … is that a problem?'

She shrugged. 'Not for me. But we don't like each other.'

'Did something happen between you two? Did you date or something?'

She snorted a bitter laugh. 'Date? Marcus date me? That's a joke. Not only is he way out of my league, I'm not even on the same planet as far as he's concerned.'

'I don't think that's true. You're really pretty, Adele.'

She scowled at me. 'That's a joke too.'

'No it's not!' I snapped. 'Why do you have such a low opinion of yourself? Do you own a mirror?'

'Of course I own a mirror. But I don't look in it if I can help it. And pretty is a word that's never been associated with me.'

'Beauty is in the eye of the beholder, Adele. You may not behold beauty when you look at your reflection, but I can assure you, others see beauty when they look at you.'

She tutted loudly.

'I mean it. Madi and I both think you're really pretty. But I will agree you don't make the most of your natural beauty. And Madi's fiancé, Tristan said he thought so too. I don't lie to people. Not even to boost their ego or make them feel better. I'm being completely honest. And I can prove it. We can call Madi now on speaker and I can ask her if she thinks you're pretty. Then you'll hear her say so yourself.'

I pulled out my phone and Adele's eyes opened wide.

'No! Please don't do that. I'd feel so embarrassed.' She smiled sheepishly again and twisted her coffee mug around in her hand. 'I ... I believe you. I'm ... I'm just not used to compliments.'

'Well you should get used to them, because if we are going to be friends, you are going to have to believe people think you're pretty.'

The smile grew wider. 'I can try.'

'Excellent! I held out my mug and clinked it with hers. 'Cheers to friendship.'

'Cheers to friendship,' she repeated.

'Now tell me, what happened before to make you wary of me?'

She let out another sigh and took in a deep breath.

'Well. There were a lot of things that caused friction between all of us. But it all came to a head when I told Marcus his wife was having an affair with his best friend, who lived next door, in your cottage.'

Eight

'Are you busy?' I asked Madi when she answered her phone an hour or so later, after I'd turned the heating on and poured myself a mug of hot chocolate from the flask Adele had kindly made me having told her about my capricious kitchen tap. 'Because you are not going to believe this, and it'll take some time for me to tell you everything.'

'Let me grab my coffee and settle on the sofa. Is this about Paul? Did something happen last night?'

'No. It's even better than that.'

'Better than Paul? What – or who, could be better than Paul?'

'Marcus and Adele. Hurry up and get settled because I'm bursting to tell you. And before you ask, Adele knows I tell you everything, and I told her I would be telling you this, so this isn't gossip or talking behind anyone's back.'

'Okay. That's good. Although, if it's juicy

I'm not sure I'd care. Right. I'm settled. Go.'

'Dad gave me a lift home and …. Oh, you don't need to know all that. Adele invited me in for coffee this morning, much to my surprise, and once we started talking, it all came tumbling out.'

'Wow! Finally. After all this time.'

I told Madi all the stuff about Adele's baking, about her low self-esteem, about her opening up regarding her feelings, about her struggling financially, about her losing her job and how she is certain Cara and possibly Jeff had been involved in some way, and then I got to the bit that had literally taken my breath away when Adele had told me.

'The guy who owned this cottage when I bought it, had been Marcus' best friend. He and Marcus had bought the cottages several years ago at the same time as Adele had bought hers. All three cottages had come up for sale when more of the land and property that was once part of Midwinter Farm was being sold off. Anyway, they all got on and soon became friends but over the course of a year or so, Adele formed a bit of a crush on Marcus.'

'You see! I knew something had happened between them,' Madi said when I had stopped for breath.

'Wait. There's more. Marcus started dating, "a stunningly beautiful woman" to use Adele's own words. Her name was Cara, and she and Adele soon became friends too, even though Adele was a little jealous of her. Marcus had no idea how Adele felt about him, and nor had Cara, as far as Adele knew.'

'They had an affair didn't they? And Cara found out.'

'No. Will you let me tell the story?'

'Okay. But hurry up.'

'Fine. Fast forward a couple of years. Cara and Marcus are now engaged, but Adele began to have doubts about Cara's friendship because Cara suddenly started saying hurtful things about Adele, not just behind her back, which Adele happened to overhear, but also to Adele's face. Things like, 'You need to watch your weight, Adele, or you'll never get a man.' Adele admitted that she started overeating when Marcus proposed to Cara. But Cara was also telling Marcus that Adele was saying hurtful things about her. About Cara, that is. Which wasn't true. But Marcus started to believe it after a while and he asked Adele to stop hurting Cara. Tensions formed between Marcus and Adele, and Cara and Adele. Marcus' best friend, Jeff said he wasn't taking sides, but then he too started being nasty to Adele.'

'Can I say something here?' Madi interrupted. 'Cara was clearly a bit of a bitch, wasn't she? Unless Adele was lying?'

'I don't think Adele was lying. Cara was a bitch, as Marcus would soon find out. Fast forward another year or so and Marcus and Cara are married. Adele wasn't invited to the wedding, but Jeff was Marcus' best man. Now Cara, Marcus, and Jeff were no longer friends with Adele and she started to feel isolated. She ate more, stayed indoors so that she didn't bump into her neighbours, and basically, her world began to fall apart. She lost her job as head baker and pastry chef at a swanky hotel a few miles away, where she had worked for several years. It's since been taken over by a hotel chain now, but anyway, she was told she was let go because there had been complaints about her food and there were rumours about her having sex with some of the guests. Something Adele said she never did and never would do. They didn't believe her because there were some photos sent anonymously to the hotel manager, of Adele having drinks at the bar with a couple of different guests. She said that's all it was. Drinks. And that those guests had invited her just for a drink.'

'Poor woman. Men can be so awful.'

'I know. Adele managed to get a job at Fairlight Bakes, but only as a waitress, because the owners do their own baking. Adele told me they are really good bakers, so I suppose that's fair enough. But this meant that she was struggling to pay her mortgage, and still is, because she's earning less than half of what she was. But she couldn't get a good reference from the hotel and she'd worked there for years so no one else would employ her without that reference.'

'Blimey. And you think you've got problems?'

'It gets worse. Adele came home early one afternoon because she wasn't feeling well, and she saw Cara and Jeff having sex. They hadn't closed the curtains because it was the afternoon and Marcus was at work and they thought Adele was too. Only a few people ever come up to the cottages on Midwinter Lane, so they probably thought they were safe. Or maybe they liked the risk of being seen. But not by Marcus, obviously. They didn't know they had been seen by Adele, who saw them at it again two days later. A few weeks later, Adele saw yet another session, but this time she managed to corner Marcus, in the car park that evening, and she told him what she'd seen and when. He didn't believe her and they argued. Jeff and Cara then told Marcus that Adele had made it up because she was obsessed with him and she wanted him for herself. Marcus believed them and told Adele that he knew what she was trying to do. He told her he'd get a restraining order against her, and they'd sue her for defamation if she spread rumours about Cara and Jeff. At the time, Marcus was a solicitor, so Adele believed he'd sue her, and she had no proof, so she stayed out of their way even more.'

'Oh my god. But would you have thought Marcus was a solicitor?'

'Nope. He isn't now. But I'll get to that. Where was I? Oh yes. By now, Adele hated Cara, Jeff and even Marcus. But one day, Marcus himself came home early and saw his wife and his best friend having sex in Jeff's sitting room, for anyone passing by to see. He stormed to the front door, and there was a massive row, which Adele heard because she was home as it was her day off. This was a few days before Christmas, two years ago. On Christmas Eve, Cara left Marcus and moved in with Jeff, next door!'

'What? She really is a bitch. And Jeff's not much better. Who needs friends like that?'

'Obviously, things were tense, and Jeff and Cara soon moved away. Jeff rented out the cottage until late last year, when he put it on the market.'

'And that's when you bought it!'

'Yep. And last Christmas, Cara had Marcus served with divorce papers. And I wondered why my neighbours weren't in the festive spirit last year, and why they didn't, and still don't, speak to one another. Oh, and apparently, Cara and Jeff are getting married this Christmas. Adele knows someone who's been invited to their wedding. So I don't think I'll be getting Marcus hanging Christmas decorations and having fun, do you?' I said, adding a bit of drama to my voice by deepening my tone. Not that it needed it. The whole sorry tale was pretty dramatic.

'Fat chance,' Madi said. 'Although … maybe that's exactly what Marcus needs. A bit of cheering up and something to take his mind off the fact that his ex-wife and his former best friend are getting married this Christmas.'

Nine

Now that I knew the story of Adele and Marcus' past, I was aware I had my work cut out to get them to become friends again, let alone more, especially as I only had twenty-two days until Christmas Eve, including today.

Marcus had accused Adele of saying hurtful things to Cara, and later, of lying. He'd ended their friendship because he believed Adele was effectively, stalking him, lying about his wife and his best friend, and trying to break up his marriage. To top that off, he'd threatened Adele with litigation.

Not exactly friendly, was it?

And although Adele had been more than a little in love with Marcus for several years, his behaviour towards her after Cara had come into their lives, had turned that love to hate.

And yet, as Adele had regaled me with their sad and sorry story, I got the feeling that the line between love and hate was wafer thin.

Perhaps there was some hope.

Or perhaps there had been too much water under that particular bridge.

Marcus had been completely wrong about Adele. It would've been good if he could have found the heart to apologise. Obviously, he was caught up in his own sadness and he might have resented Adele for being the one who had first made him aware of his wife's infidelity, which he had chosen not to believe. He might have felt foolish for allowing himself to be blind to the betrayal by his wife and his best friend.

Yet, without knowing any of their history, I had seen how much Marcus and Adele had in common. And Adele had said they were such good friends before he had met Cara.

Was there any way that I could get them to at least, share the gift of friendship again this Christmas?

I would have to give the matter some serious thought. I'd discuss it more with Madi.

And maybe with Berry too. I might also ask Paul for his opinion, merely to get the male perspective, although I wouldn't tell either of them all the details, or give them names. That wouldn't be fair to Adele and

Marcus. I'd simply tell them that two friends had fallen out when the partner of one of them had had an affair with a third friend, and that one of the first two had revealed the affair. Hopefully, that would sort of explain it.

But for now I needed to make some Christmas decorations.

The cottage was lovely and warm, the heating having been on ever since I'd come home from Adele's, and I had enough hot chocolate to last me for a while yet. Adele had kindly offered to make me a fresh flask later, or to make tea if I would prefer that.

Life was strange sometimes and often threw us surprises. If I hadn't spent the night with my parents, and if Dad hadn't given me a lift, and if I hadn't stopped on the wooden bridge and marvelled at nature, I might not have seen Adele open her front door, and I wouldn't have waved, and I wouldn't have been invited in for coffee.

That string of events had meant that Adele had poured her heart out to me, and in doing so, we had finally struck up a friendship.

I munched on one of her delicious cinnamon cookies. She'd given me a plastic container with enough of them to last me for a week. As I savoured the second one and washed it down with some more of her equally delicious hot chocolate, I had an idea.

Adele had told me she was struggling financially. She needed extra cash; I was thinking of taking on some help. Would she be interested in helping me with my Midwinter Cottage Decorations? I knew she worked shifts in Fairlight Bakes, but I was happy with someone who needed flexible hours. I'd run it by her later. But I'd mention it to Madi first to see what she thought.

What Adele should really do was set up her own small business, selling her scrumptious cookies locally. She could have a market stall like Berry and me. And maybe sell them online, too. I didn't know what was involved with edible goods, but I was sure Adele could soon find out, or might even know already.

I could offer to sell a few batches on my stall on Thursday and again on Saturday. Christmas cookies and Christmas decorations went together like Santa and his reindeer.

And then I had another idea. I could buy several batches from Adele and give them as Christmas presents. That would help both of us.

And what if...?

'Wow!' I said aloud. 'Ideas are coming to me like snowflakes on a wintry day.'

Although there wasn't any sign yet of the

snow that had been forecast. But it was only Monday.

Which reminded me. I had told Mum I would call the heating guy to see if there was any chance of an earlier appointment. I knew it was a long shot but it was worth a try. I'd do that after lunch.

I glanced out of my sitting room window and saw Marcus trudging across the bridge. I jumped to my feet and raced to the front door, flinging it open in such a hurry and with more force than I realised. It hit the rubber door stop on the hall wall, bounced back, and knocked me forward. I almost lost all the cookies on the plate I was holding.

Thankfully, I didn't. But Marcus gave me an odd sort of look as he strode up his path, having clearly quickened his pace, no doubt in an attempt to avoid me.

'Hi Marcus!'

I smiled my sweetest smile as I stepped out onto my lawn and walked towards the fence, the red noses of my reindeer slipper boots, lighting up and flashing with each step I took.

A tight smile tugged at his mouth as his eyes travelled to my feet. 'Hello, Noelle.'

'I thought you might like a cinnamon cookie. I've got loads and they're so scrummy.'

Did his gaze dart towards Adele's

cottage? Or did I imagine that?

'Homemade?' he asked, eyeing them with longing as he walked towards me.

'Uh-huh.'

That wasn't a lie. They were homemade. Just not homemade by me.

'Then, yes please. I haven't had a cinnamon cookie since ... for a long time.'

He reached out and took one.

'Take the plate,' I said, and then grinned. 'Just the plate. Not the cookies. Only joking. Take the plate and the cookies. I have more.'

He laughed and for the first time since I'd met him I noticed how lovely his eyes were. They were a greenish-brown with sprinkles of gold. And his mouth was the perfect shape and size. I could see why Adele had fallen for him.

'Thank you,' he said, taking a bite of the cookie in his hand. His eyes lit up even more and his entire face brightened, and then it was gone and a frown formed between his brows.

'What's wrong? Don't you like it?' How could anyone not like it?

'It's ... it's perfect,' he said, a hint of sadness in his voice. 'Did you make them?'

'Here. Take the rest.'

I held the plate out to him and he eyed it with suspicion.

'Noelle? Did you make them or not?' The

softness in his voice was gone and there was a hard edge to it, and to his eyes now, as he stared at me.

'Does it matter who made them? It's Christmas, Marcus. It's the season of goodwill. Of forgiveness and love. Of friendship and good deeds.'

'Of betrayal and divorce papers. Of lies, and deceit, and of moving on and leaving people heartbroken. Thanks, Noelle. But I think I'll pass.'

He tossed the rest of the biscuit back onto the plate and turned and marched away.

'Marcus? Marcus!'

My appeals fell on deaf ears and he slammed his front door to make his message clear.

I hadn't thought it would be easy, but I hadn't expected that.

I turned and went back inside, peeking towards Adele's and hoping she was in her kitchen and hadn't seen what had just transpired.

Ten

'I think I might've blown it,' I told Madi after I'd drunk all the hot chocolate, and eaten four of the cinnamon biscuits, having thrown the half-eaten one in the bin.

'What are we talking about?' Madi asked, giggling like a schoolgirl. 'I need to get some context.'

'Marcus and Adele, and my matchmaking skills. Or to be precise, failed matchmaking skills.'

'Ah right. Is this going to be a long call?'

'Am I boring you already?'

'You could never bore me. I just wanted to ascertain if I should get myself a drink or not.'

'That depends on your response to what I tell you.'

'Hold on. Tristan! If you're in the kitchen, would you be a darling and make me a cup of tea, please?'

'Of course, sweetheart,' Tristan yelled

back, although I could only just hear him on my end of the call. 'Say hello to Noelle.'

'How did he know it was me?'

'No one else calls me,' she laughed.

I knew that wasn't true, and I laughed too. 'I do keep calling rather a lot recently, don't I?'

'I love our chats. Call me as often as you like.'

'Thanks for being such a wonderful friend.'

'Thank you for being such a wonderful friend too. Now let's move on. What's happened?'

I told her about biscuitgate, as I was going to think of it. All failed plans had to have a name.

'I see. That was a cunning plan, but I know where you went wrong. His wife lied. His best friend lied. He probably still believes Adele lied in some way. And now you've lied too, as far as he's concerned. I would say he's had enough of liars, wouldn't you?'

'I suppose so. I didn't think of that.'

'What I think you should've done was to have said that Adele gave them to you, and that although they're delicious, you're watching your weight because you're going on a date with the man of your dreams, and that he ... Marcus, I mean, not your dream man, would be doing you a favour if he took the biscuits, because you're not the sort of person who would throw away such yummy food, or who would ever want to upset someone, or hurt their feelings.'

'Where were you when I needed you? I should've called you first. But he came home unexpectedly and I acted on the spur of the moment.'

'Which is probably what Cara said two years ago,' Madi quipped. 'Sorry. Poor taste.'

'But probably true. How can I make this better?'

'Well ... he doesn't know that you know about his past, does he? You could go round right now and bang on the door and demand an explanation. But in a friendly way. Say you don't understand his reaction or his comments and that if you have upset him in some way, you're very sorry. Because you're not the sort of person ... etc., etc., and give him a Christmas decoration as well. One of those snowmen ones that are holding out their hearts. Everyone goes all gooey over those.'

'You're a genius. But wait. Isn't that lying? What if he then finds out I did know about his past?'

'Worry about that when the time comes. You could tell him you found out the same day from Adele.'

'So still lie, you mean?'

'It's a white lie, not a bad lie. And it's only a lie if someone finds out it's not the truth.'

'Should I be worried?' Tristan asked, laughing in the background.

'I would never lie to you, darling,' Madi said, and I could hear lips meeting lips in a kiss. 'Thanks for the tea.'

'Thanks for the kiss,' said Tristan. 'Catch you later, Noelle.'

'Bye, Tristan.'

'I love that man to bits,' said Madi, swooning loudly.

'And he loves you to bits too. Right. I'm going round to see Marcus. Wish me luck.'

'Good luck. Call me after.'

'Bye After,' I joked.

Madi groaned in an amused fashion and rang off.

I slid the remaining biscuits into one of the transparent plastic bags I used for my Christmas decorations, found one of the snowmen Madi had suggested, and, after putting on my coat and boots, I headed to End Cottage and rang the doorbell.

'Oh. It's you.' Marcus didn't seem pleased to see me.

'I come bearing gifts. And an apology. Although I think you owe me an apology too. I just offered you some biscuits and they weren't poisoned or anything so I don't understand your comments or your reaction.

Adele made the biscuits and they're absolutely delicious, but the thing is, I need to watch my weight because I'm going on a date and I'm not the sort of person who would throw away such yummy food, or who would ever want to upset someone, or hurt their feelings. So I offered them to you. That's it. I've tried my hardest to be your friend. Your friend and nothing more. I don't fancy you or anything, so don't worry about that, but I would like to know why you feel it's okay to be rude and unpleasant and frankly, unkind.'

He raised his brows and his mouth dropped open.

'Oh, and I also brought you this,' I added, holding out the snowman decoration. 'I did make this one. I have my own small business making Christmas decorations. I think I told you that. Anyway. I don't know if you have a tree. I don't have mine yet. But this goes on a tree. Or a door handle. Or anywhere, really. Or you can give it to someone else if it's not your thing.'

We stared at one another for what felt like for ever, and then to my astonishment, he laughed. It was just a quick burst, but again that lovely light popped into his eyes.

He took a deep breath and smiled. 'I've just made some tea. Would you like a cup?'

'Oh yes please! My boiler's playing up,

and so is my tap in the kitchen, so I'm all over the place right now. Sorry. Tea would be lovely.'

He stepped aside to let me in and I gasped as I walked along the hall. Again, End Cottage was, or would've once been, a similar layout to mine, and to Adele's, but they couldn't be more different style-wise, if they tried.

Apart from the hall, the downstairs of End Cottage was all open plan, sleek lines, expensive furniture and furnishings, artwork on the walls, a designer kitchen I would've died for, and glass, sliding doors the width of the back wall. There was also a TV the size of a spaceship on one wall, with surround sound speakers as stylish as the rest of the furniture.

'Crikey. This is posh.'

'Erm. Thanks. I think.'

I laughed at his uncertainty. 'That was a compliment. It's gorgeous. But I'm surprised by the sliding doors. Sorry. That's not a criticism. I meant no offence.'

'None taken. We ... I was going to have bifolds, but our ... my architect suggested sliding doors instead.' He gave a small cough and took a breath as though he was resetting himself. 'Apparently bifolding doors let out more heat and aren't as good as everyone seems to believe. That was his opinion, but he was a friend. A friend I trust. So I went with his suggestion. One of the many things that infuriated my ex-wife. Before she was my ex. Please take a seat.'

He pointed at a sumptuous looking chair and I sank into the comfy cushions while he poured me a cup of tea from an expensive looking porcelain teapot.

'Have you lived here long?' I asked before realising that I hadn't aired my surprise that he had been married. Oh well. That ship had sailed.

'Yes. Possibly too long. But I love this cottage and I always have. At least, for most of the time I've lived here. Milk?' A matching milk jug hovered in his hand over the cup.'

'Yes please. No sugar. I'm sweet enough.'

He raised his brows. 'That speech wasn't terribly sweet. And I'm not convinced all of it was true. But the snowman is delightful. I believe you mean well and you're a genuine person. I apologise for my bad manners but you hit a nerve, I'm afraid. Just tell me the truth. How much do you know about my past?'

I could've lied. But as he handed me the porcelain cup and saucer, I decided complete honesty was the way to go.

'Thanks for the tea. I love this porcelain tea set.'

He sat in the chair opposite me and gave

me a strange look.

'A wedding gift from my parents. One I decided not to smash to smithereens when I discovered my wife was shagging my best friend.'

I choked on the sip I'd taken and had to cough to clear my throat.

'Too honest for you?' he asked with the hint of a sardonic smile.

I shook my head. 'Brutal honesty is sometimes best. So I'll be honest with you. I had absolutely no idea about anything in your past. I didn't even know you were once a solicitor until today. And the only reason I found out any of it was because Adele was upset when I arrived back here this morning and she invited me in for coffee. She's been unwell and she's clearly run down, although she said she feels better today. But I think she's been holding it all in for so long that once we started talking, it all came pouring out.'

His expression changed to one I couldn't quite fathom.

'Today? You only heard about it all today?'

'Yes. Well let's be honest again. Neither you or Adele have been brimming over with friendship and welcome, have you? And neither of you have been keen to chat, or to open up about yourselves. Now I think I understand why. I'm so sorry you had to go through that.'

He snorted another sardonic laugh. 'I bet my name was mud. Adele hates me. But I suppose I can't blame her.'

'Actually, she didn't say anything bad about you, really. But she was upset that you didn't believe her. It's none of my business, I know, but you two seem to have so much in common and it's so sad that you were once good friends but now you don't speak to one another.'

His face hardened and his jaw tightened and I wondered if he might throw me out, but then that light came back into his eyes and his smile was wistful, as was the small sigh that escaped him.

'We were good friends once. Really close friends. I almost asked her out. But Jeff said he thought it might ruin our friendship, so I didn't. And then I met Cara.' His fingers turned white as he gripped the handle of his cup so tightly, I thought it might break. 'Too much information. Sorry. But I shouldn't have listened to Jeff, should I? Things might be so different now if I'd followed my ... but it's too late for that. Would you like to hear my side of this sordid little tale? Or did Adele tell you everything you want to know?'

'I'd like to hear your side too, if you want to tell me. But that's entirely up to you. It won't change anything as far as I'm concerned. I want to be friends with both you and Adele, if that's possible. And what's in the past is in the past as far as I'm concerned. Unless it affects the present and the future. But I feel I must say one thing. Two things actually. I do genuinely believe that Adele only had your interests and your happiness at heart when she told you about your wife and your best friend. Those aren't her words, they're mine. She said she had feelings for you and admitted she was jealous of Cara, but I think it was Cara who was the bitch, not Adele. And the second thing is, it's never too late to do anything. Whether that's to follow your heart, or to follow your dreams, or to fly to the moon and back. Okay that last one might not be so easy. But if there is breath in your body and hope in your heart, then it's not too late.'

He eyed me over his cup and remained silent for several seconds.

'Thank you for that. I will tell you my side of it all one day. But not today, I think. I know I should probably be over it by now, but the cold hard truth is, I'm not. My ex-wife is marrying my former best friend this Christmas and to say I'm a little upset is possibly an understatement.'

'These things take as long as they take. Is that why you don't like Christmas?'

'Who said I don't like Christmas? Surely not Adele?'

'No! But ... well, you didn't put any decorations up last year, and you didn't thank me for my card, or send me one, so I sort of assumed.'

He nodded. 'I see. Yes. I apologise for not doing that. The card thing, I mean. That was rude. I loved Christmas. So did Adele. Jeff and my ex could take it or leave it. But Jeff took my wife instead. Two years ago at Christmas. She moved into your cottage with him on Christmas Eve, so that Christmas was fun, as you can imagine. I did have decorations up that year, but I tore them all down on New Year's Eve. Last Christmas, she sent me divorce papers, so that was another fun Christmas. I didn't bother to buy new decorations, as you noticed. And this year, when I thought things might start to get better, I heard she and Jeff are getting married on Christmas Eve. Who, in their right mind, gets married on Christmas Eve? So, I think we've established that's it's highly unlikely that End Cottage will be decked in boughs of holly and twinkling lights this year either. Hmm. I think I might need something stronger than tea. Several somethings in fact. Luckily I have the afternoon off. Want to join me?'

I could hear Mum's voice saying,

'Drinking alcohol at lunchtime? And on a Monday? Surely not?'

'Absolutely,' I said. 'I haven't been drunk since Saturday night. Oh wait. I also had a few too many yesterday afternoon. Although I wasn't drunk. But I'll only have one.'

Where had I heard that before?

He raised a brow and reminded me a little of my dad.

'Do you have a drink problem?'

'No. It's no problem at all. It slides down rather nicely. Sorry. I shouldn't joke about that. I have been drinking a little more than usual over the last few months, but I don't think I have a problem.'

'Isn't that what people with a problem would say?'

'Yep. Probably. But seriously, I don't. And I will just have one drink with you. A glass of wine if you have some, please.'

'One glass of wine coming up.' He opened the biggest wine fridge I'd ever seen outside of a restaurant. 'Any preference?'

'Cold, white, and wet.'

He grinned. 'A true connoisseur.'

'You'd better believe it.'

He poured a large glass and handed it to me. 'Only one,' he said. 'I'll drink the rest.'

'Only one,' I replied and took a large mouthful. 'Oh my god! That's like the nectar of the gods.'

'It's not a bad year.' He sat opposite me again and leant forward in his chair. 'That was the year I got married. As you can tell, I like to wallow in self-pity and literally, drown my sorrows. Or maybe drown in my sorrows. Cheers,' he said, clinking my glass with his.

'Cheers,' I replied, sipping my wine and savouring the deliciousness of it, as he knocked his back in three large gulps and then refilled his glass.

'Was that bit about you going on a date, true?' He grinned at me over the rim of his glass. 'Asking for a friend. The bit about you needing to watch your weight clearly isn't.'

I shifted uncomfortably. 'I do need to watch my weight. I've been stuffing my face with Adele's biscuits. Now those I could get addicted to.'

'There're certainly delicious, I agree. I knew as soon as I took that first bite that they were her biscuits. No one makes cinnamon biscuits – or any biscuits, like Adele. And the date?'

'The date? Oh, the date! Erm. Not entirely. There is a guy I really like and I think he likes me too. But he's just split up from his girlfriend. Literally, on Saturday night, and he's also the older brother of a good friend of mine, so I don't know if it's going to be a bit weird, or even if he'll ask me out.'

'He'll ask you out. Unless my friend does first.'

I gave a little gasp. 'Erm. Please don't take this the wrong way. And please don't take it personally, but as lovely as you are, and as much as I want to be your friend, I ... I don't think we would work. You're not my type and I'm not yours. Not that I know what your type is. But I'm sure it's not me. Is that okay? Are we good?'

He was trying to hide his laughter. I could see it in his face. Was the man teasing me? The more I said, the more he struggled to hide it, until he finally let rip and roared with laughter.

'I apologise,' he said when I glared at him. 'Seriously I do. But oh, Noelle, you're the best. You really are. You've cheered me up no end. As for you being my type, well, I think you could be, because you're beautiful. You're funny. You're witty and intelligent. You have your own business and you own your own home. I love all those things about you. But I was genuinely asking for a friend. Do you like kids?'

I raised my brows in mock horror, delighted that he'd said such lovely things about me but equally delighted that he wasn't asking me out.

'I've never dated anyone more than a few years younger than me, so if that's what you're suggesting, it's a hard no from me.'

He roared again and his body shook with laughter. 'No. My friend is thirty-nine but he has a daughter who is eight. He's a widower. He has his own business and he's in high demand, so he doesn't get a chance to go out and meet women, what with working long hours and then wanting to spend all his free time with his daughter.'

'Oh I see. You're serious?'

'I'm serious. I'm not his pimp or anything, and he'd kill me if he knew I was telling you this. But you and he would be perfect for one another. If I could find a way to arrange a casual meeting, would you be interested? Or has this other man already stolen your heart? Because my friend wouldn't date a woman who was also seeing someone else.'

'Erm. I'm not sure. Can I think about it? Paul is – that's the man I like – gorgeous and I know him fairly well. I'm not sure I'd be up for a blind date. Do you have a photo of him?'

'Yes. I carry one close to my heart at all times.' He threw me a playful look. 'No. I don't think I do. We're not the sort of guys who pose for photos. And he's not on social media. As you can see, there are no photos on my walls. Not even of my parents. Although there is a room upstairs that has several photos of my ex and I throw darts at them every night before I go to bed.' He emptied his glass again and refilled it. 'Can I tempt you?'

'With another glass? Or to throw darts at the photos of your ex? Because that sounds like fun. But I think I'll say no to both. Thanks.'

He grinned. 'Are looks important to you?'

'Not that important, no. But I like to see a man's eyes. You can tell a lot about a person from their eyes.'

'I agree. And in case there is any doubt in your mind, I don't have a room filled with photos of my ex, and I don't throw darts at them because they don't exist. I will admit I did burn them all though. The night she moved into your cottage.'

'I know you said you're not completely over her yet, but I think you're in better shape than you believe you are.'

'I hope you're right.'

'And having said that, I think it might be weird going on a date with a friend of yours. Thanks for the offer, but if it's all the same to you, I think I'll say no. This has been fun. But I really must get back because I'm supposed to be making Christmas decorations for my business. Plus, I need to phone my plumber to see if he can come any sooner than tomorrow. I've got problems with my boiler, and the tap in my kitchen thinks it's a shower. Don't ask.' I got to my feet and he did so too. 'Anyway, the wine was heavenly and I'd love to know what it is.' I handed him the glass and he took it. 'Oh, and before I go, would you mind if I gave you a piece of advice?'

He turned and walked away, but he glanced over his shoulder and said, 'Please do,' as he put the glass on the counter and then walked towards the wine fridge once again, returning moments later with two bottles of chilled white wine. 'For you. And possibly to drink with your date.'

'Are you sure?'

He nodded and smiled.

'Thank you.' I glanced down at the labels and gave a little gasp. 'I ... I can't accept these. I may not be a connoisseur but I know that this is bloody expensive wine. Eye-wateringly expensive, in fact.'

Even my Mum had heard of Montrachet. A white burgundy considered to be one of the best white wines in the world. And these were aged Premier Cru wines. I had once been in a restaurant when someone had ordered an aged bottle of a Montrachet Premier Cru, and a friend who worked there told me prices ranged from the hundreds to the thousands depending on the year.

'No. Not eye-wateringly so, and not

really bloody, either. Not for what they are. But I'll agree they're not cheap. Isn't that what money is for though? To spend it on nice things and to make ourselves happy. And you did give me a wonderful gift, so please accept the wine in the spirit in which it's offered. One of friendship.'

'I gave you biscuits made by someone else and a snowman to hang on a Christmas tree that you don't even have, and probably won't be getting. It's hardly the same, is it?'

'Gifts shouldn't be about how much they cost. It's about the sentiment, not the price. And besides, those weren't the only gifts you've given me. You might not realise this but you've made me laugh more today than I have done for some time. Plus, you've made me see the light on a matter that has only been dark until now. Sometimes it takes someone new to come into your life to make you see what a prat you've been. Thank you for making me see I'm a prat.'

'Oh, you're very welcome. And now for that advice. Adele is not your enemy. But you were in the wrong when you accused her of lying and I think you should apologise for that. I don't know if you can be friends again but I hope that you can. You said yourself you were close. A true friend, like true love, is hard to come by and it's worth making an effort to keep that friendship, or to reignite it. Apologise for what you said and did. I'm pretty sure she'll apologise to you for causing you the hurt that she did, but she was being honest. Right that's it. Do I still get to keep both bottles of this exorbitantly expensive, posh white wine? Or do you want them back?'

He had been staring at me as I spoke but now he smiled and to my surprise he leant forward and kissed me on the cheek.

'You get to keep them both. And you might find you get some more between now and Christmas. 'Tis the season, after all.' He winked at me. 'Now get out of here and let me get drunk. I'm going to stalk my ex on social media for the very last time and then I'm going to man up and get over her, once and for all. I'm sure I must have some darts somewhere.'

Eleven

I was going to send Adele a text to give her a heads up that she might receive a visit from Marcus at some stage. And also, that he might be drunk if it was today. But then I thought it might be best to let it be a surprise. And also, he might not go to see her, and that would only make her more upset.

But then again, if there was even the slightest chance that someone I liked might turn up on my doorstep, unannounced, I'd like to look my best. So eventually I decided I had to tell her.

'I'm not saying he will,' I said. 'But I'm not saying he won't. All I'm saying is that we spoke for a long time today and he seemed to ... mellow. Actually, he seemed to care about you. I think there's a chance you could become friends once again.'

'Really? What did he say? But do I want to be friends with someone who could think I would behave like that?'

'That's entirely up to you. All I'll say is that I believe you still like him, deep down. Maybe even more than like him. And the woman was his wife, after all. It would've been a bit unfair of him to take your side against her when you had no proof and the wife and best friend denied it. Think about it and see how you feel. But don't let it upset you if he doesn't turn up. He's still upset about his best friend and his wife betraying him. This might take some time.'

'I understand. And I promise I'll think about it.'

She looked rather excited and I hoped I hadn't caused her even more heartache by getting involved.

'There's something else I wanted to ask you. Would you be interested in helping me make my Christmas decorations? I've got orders coming out of my ears and I've been thinking of taking someone on, part time and on flexible hours. I'll pay the going rate.'

'Are you sure?' She looked doubtful. 'You haven't just made this up because of what I told you about my finances, have you? I don't want charity.'

'Cross my heart, I haven't made this up. It's the honest truth. I could really do with some help. And having the person live next door is a godsend. It means I don't have to lug stock back and forth. If you're unsure, we could give it a try and see how we get on. If we both hate it, and can't work together, or if you don't enjoy it, then we can forget it and still be friends. Deal?'

The furrow between her brows slowly melted away and she smiled.

'Deal. When do you want me to start?'

'As soon as you're feeling better.'

'I'm feeling better already. You've made my day, Noelle.'

'Then let's start as soon as my boiler is fixed, which should be tomorrow, with any luck.'

'Perfect. Erm. I think I might go and have a quick shower. I've been baking all morning and I'm covered in flour.'

It was obvious she wanted to have a shower in case Marcus turned up, and I really hoped he would.

'Oh that reminds me. I love your biscuits so much and I want to buy some to give as presents. I was also thinking that you should consider setting up your own business because even Marcus said your biscuits are the best.'

'Marcus said that? Today?'

'Yep. I gave him some when I saw him. So I'd like to buy some more, please.'

'Buy them? You can have them for free.'

'Nope. This is business, Adele. Work out how much they cost to make and how much profit you want and then look online to see what other biscuit makers charge to make sure you don't price them too cheap. I'll see you tomorrow.'

She gave me a quick hug and I dashed back to my cottage feeling that it had been a much better day than I'd expected.

I'd only been in a few minutes and in my joyful state, I'd forgotten about my tap. I turned it on and got completely drenched from the top of my head to my trousers. Even my reindeer head slipper boots were wet. I was on my way upstairs to get a towel and get changed when the doorbell rang.

I thought it was probably Adele. Or possibly Marcus. So I didn't worry about how I might look as I flung open the door.

'That bloody tap has just ... Oh. ... Ooooh.'

I hadn't meant to say that second and rather swoony, oh, and certainly not aloud. But it sort of drifted out of me as my eyes beheld the gorgeous hunk of a man standing at my front door, and my gaze travelled up and down his seemingly perfect body.

'Marcus called and told me I had to come here today, as a favour to him,' he said, as his gaze scanned me from my head to my toes, but not in the same appreciative way that I knew my eyes were scanning him.

'Did he?' I said, my voice all soft and

dreamy. I coughed to clear my throat. 'I mean, did he? Why? Oh no. You're not my blind date, are you? Look. I'm sure you're lovely … and I can see that you're very handsome. Marcus didn't mention that. But I did say that I thought it would be best if we didn't date. I don't have an issue with kids. In fact, I like them. But if things didn't work out, it would just be awkward.' I shook my head slowly. 'And you have no idea what I'm talking about, do you?'

'Not a clue. I'm here about a tap and a boiler. Have you been trying to fix them yourself?' His expression reminded me that I was drenched. 'I think you've drowned your reindeer. Aren't their noses supposed to flash?'

'What? Oh yes. Erm. Sorry, but why did Marcus tell you, you had to come here today?'

'Faulty boiler? Leaky tap? Ring any bells?'

'Several. But who are you?'

'Well I'm not Father Christmas. Do I need to give you any other clues?'

'Erm. Look. I'm not trying to be difficult so there's no need for sarcasm. I just don't know why Marcus called you. He didn't tell me he was calling a plumber, which is what I assume you are.'

'Give the girl a candy cane.'

I ignored his facetious remark. 'I have a plumber booked for tomorrow. Although I did say I was going to call him and see if he could get here any sooner even though he said he couldn't.'

'It's the season for miracles. Here I am.' He held out his arms in a sort of theatrical gesture. 'Ta dah. Now are you going to let me in?'

'No. Not until you tell me who you are. You could be anyone for all I know. And where are your tools if you're a plumber?'

He raised his brows. 'I'm a heating engineer and plumber. And I told you Marcus called me. My tools are in my van. I don't carry them around with me until I know which tools I will need. I might have to go and buy some parts before I even start, and I don't leave my tools lying around in case someone trips over them and sues me. Marcus told me about that. I'm the man you want. The one you called yesterday. I'm Alec Richman. And I have to say I'm only here today because Marcus is a good mate. But I've got places to be and people to see so either let me in or I'll leave and come back another time. It's up to you.'

'You're ... you're Alec Richman?'

'Yep.'

My gaze took him in again and I felt my mouth fall open but I quickly composed myself. I'd imagined Paul when I'd pictured Alec but this man made Paul look ordinary.

Alec had the sort of sandy-golden-blond hair, and suntanned skin that made him look as if he lived on a surfer's paradise beach. His smile was devastating, and his teeth were white but naturally white, not blitzed and bleached to within an inch of their lives. His blue eyes were the colour of a hot summer day, and his jaw was firm and clean-shaven. He had the sort of body any athlete would kill for, and any woman would want to wake up next to. This man was the perfect package. Looks-wise, at least.

'Why didn't you just say who you were?'

'And spoil all that fun?'

'You're not at all what I was expecting.'

'I get that a lot. Sorry to disappoint. But there it is. Now, what's it to be? In or out?'

'What! Oh, in. Yes. Definitely in. And I'm not disappointed. Just surprised. Thank you for coming sooner.'

'I'm just glad I'm not your blind date, because if you give a plumber you've called this much of a hard time, I'd hate to see the sort of grilling you give a potential boyfriend. And you might want to go and wash your face. You've got black streaks running down your cheeks. Point me in the direction of the boiler, or the tap, before you go and do that, and I'll crack on.'

My hands shot to my face and my cheeks burned with embarrassment.

'The kitchen is that way. The boiler's in the utility room which you'll see when you're in the kitchen.'

'Thanks. Any chance of a cup of tea? I'm parched and as I said, I dashed up here because Marcus told me to. I should be on my tea break now.'

'Yes. If you're willing to be the one to turn on the tap. That's how this happened.'

He grinned at me and I hurried upstairs.

I was mortified by my reflection.

Why had Marcus called my plumber and told him to come here today? And how did Marcus know which plumber I'd called? I'm sure I hadn't told him.

I wished I'd taken Marcus' number as I had done Adele's, then I could have called and asked him.

I dashed into the shower and had the fastest wash in history, spending time on my face to remove the black streaks. I wasn't sure what they were as I hadn't put mascara on today.

Then I remembered I'd been painting the snowmen's top hats with black paint. I must've got some on my face and when that tap soaked me, the paint had run down my cheeks. Luckily it washed off.

At least I could now make myself more

presentable and I stepped out of the shower smiling at the thought of Alec saying, 'you look lovely,' or something similar when he saw my transformation from drowned rat to reasonably pretty woman.

Well a girl could dream, couldn't she?

What I had definitely not expected was for Alec to see me naked.

I'm not sure who screamed the loudest.

'Shit! I'm so sorry,' he yelled, taking more than a moment or two before he looked away and turned around.

'Fuc–' Thankfully, I didn't finish that profanity. Saying F... me, might have made him think I was giving him an invitation, not that I was so startled at finding him in my bedroom that I had used a phrase I'd only used once before in my life.

'What the hell are you doing in my bedroom?' I questioned his back after I'd grabbed the towel I'd foolishly left on my bed.

'I was coming to turn off the rads. I had no idea you were taking a shower. I did call out as I came up the stairs and I thought you heard me because I'd said, 'Shout now if you're not decent.' And I couldn't hear any water running, so how was I to know you'd be naked? I suggested you wash your face, not your whole body. But I will say you have a really good body. Your blind date guy is in for a treat.'

'What! How dare you. Firstly, you should've waited for my reply. Secondly, you should've looked away the moment you saw I was naked. Thirdly, I don't sleep with men on first dates. And I said I wasn't going on a date with you ... him ... anyway.'

My voice had grown louder and more shrieky with each sentence and I was glad his back was turned and he couldn't see my face.

'Okay, okay. I'm sorry. And you're right. I should've looked away immediately. I don't know why I didn't because despite what you might think I am a gentleman. Usually. But ... I think I was as surprised as you were, and then ... I think I was just mesmerised or something. As I said, you have a really good body. A *really good* body.'

'Thank you!' I hissed. But inside I was thrilled. This gorgeous man thought I had a really good body.

His phone rang and he answered it immediately.

And broke my heart and shattered my dreams with just two words.

'Hi sweetheart,' he said.

So Alec obviously had a girlfriend. Or a fiancée. Or a wife.

Okay, he hadn't actually broken my heart or shattered any dreams. I'd only met the guy a few minutes ago. But I had thought

Paul set my heart and body on fire. This man had set my heart and my body and my soul ablaze the second I opened my front door.

'I can't talk right now,' he continued, his voice soft and loving. 'I'm in the middle of something. But I'll see you very soon and yes, we can snuggle up on the sofa and watch your favourite movie tonight. Love you, sweetheart. Bye for now.'

I wondered what she looked like naked. Did he tell her she had a really good body too?

He coughed. 'Are you decent? Can I turn around?'

'I suppose so.'

I had the towel wrapped around me, but when he turned to face me, I may as well have been naked once again because his eyes slowly grazed my skin and it was as if he was caressing me with his bare hands. Tingles and quivers of delight raced up and down my arms and legs and everywhere in between.

His voice sounded as though it was dragged over coals. 'Can I turn off the radiator, please?'

Mine was almost breathless. 'Yes.'

I managed to pull myself together and I sounded more serious and detached when I added, 'And then, in case you think of coming back to do something else, I'm giving you notice now that I'll be getting dressed.'

'Do something ...? Oh right. No. Just need to turn off the rads for now. In every room.'

He had to walk past me to get to the radiator in my bedroom and although we didn't touch, I could feel the heat from his body and smell his aftershave. When our eyes met for an instant, I actually considered dropping the towel. And unless I was completely misreading the look in his eyes, I think he was hoping that I would.

At first, that made me even more aroused, but then I remembered that phone call and it was as though I'd had another cold shower.

Would he cheat on his partner? If so, he wasn't the kind of man I'd want to take to my bed.

I turned away but I could feel his eyes on me and, even though it shouldn't have, it made me feel sexier and more desirable than I'd felt in many years.

Twelve

'Are you serious?'

Madi couldn't believe it when I told her about my talk with Marcus, or that I'd offered Adele a job, but what really blew her mind was when I told her about Alec Richman and the bedroom incident.

'Deadly serious. I've never experienced anything like it before. It was as if a magnet was pulling us together. And the lust and longing I felt were out of this world. Talk about animal instincts. Honestly, if we'd been in that bedroom for even a second longer, I think we'd have been having sex. And we'd still be having it now. Several hours later. There's something about him. Don't ask me what because he was rude and sarcastic and he's got a girlfriend, fiancée, or wife, so he would've been an absolute bastard if he had had sex with me. But even so.' I let out a long and wistful sigh. 'I've never wanted a man as much in my entire life.'

'Crikey. That's worrying. You said he's coming back to finish the job. Did you mean the heating, or something more personal?' She laughed.

'Hilarious. I had to stay out of his way while he was here and I'll have to do the same when he comes back, because believe me, if he looks at me again, the way he looked at me in my bedroom, I think I'd throw myself at him.'

'Perhaps you should ask Adele to stay with you while he's there. You said she's starting tomorrow, didn't you?'

'She is. And maybe I should.'

'So is Paul ancient history now then?'

'Paul who? That was a joke. I don't know. And that's another problem. If Paul asks me out, I think I should say yes. Because whatever this is with Alec, it can't go anywhere, can it? And it'd only be a fling for him, and I think I'm ready for something more. Something serious. Something lasting. I want what you've got with Tristan. Minus the apples and the cider. No wait. I'll have the cider too.'

'I think you should go out with Paul. I don't know why he hasn't asked you yet though. Maybe he feels he needs to leave it a few days and not rush into another relationship right away.'

'Maybe. And that makes sense. I'll see

Berry on Thursday so I might try to find out what's going on, and perhaps I'll drop a hint and see what she says.'

'That's a great idea. Are you going to stay at your parents' house again tonight?'

'Yep. The heating won't work properly until Alec gets the new timer and does something else that I can't remember, because all I could think about when he was telling me what was wrong with it, and also with the tap, was that he had come to bed eyes, and how gorgeous and sexy his mouth was and how much I wanted him to kiss me. All over. Every single inch of me.'

'You've got it bad.'

'I know. There should be a vaccine for this.'

'Well, speaking of kissing someone all over, Tristan has just walked in with our fish and chips, so I'll love you and leave you. Call me tomorrow with all the details.'

'Love you both. Bye for now.'

I rang off and glanced out of my sitting room window, just in time to spot Marcus. I was going to rush outside and ask him why he'd called my plumber and how he'd got the man to come to me today, but I realised he was walking past my cottage and was therefore either popping to the post box, which for some reason seemed unlikely, especially as it appeared that he had a wine bottle in one hand, or he was on his way to Adele's.

I got rather excited until it struck me that his walk was unsteady.

Was the man drunk?

Was it wise to go and have a chat with Adele after all this time, if so?

Or had he needed to be tipsy to pluck up the courage to go and apologise after nearly two years of not speaking to her?

I watched surreptitiously until he made it to the front door and then I waited for a few minutes longer to be certain she had let him in.

I smiled to myself when it was obvious that she had and I kept my fingers crossed that my work here was done. At least as far as getting Adele and Marcus to talk to one another and to be friends with me. There might still be a way to go until Adele and Marcus would be best friends again. And maybe something more.

I knew Adele still had feelings for Marcus, however much she might try to convince herself those feelings were of hatred. And Marcus had told me himself that he had once thought of asking her out but that his so-called best friend at the time, Jeff, had persuaded him not to. He'd said that I had made him see something in a new light; something that had only been dark until now. Was that something the realisation that what he felt for Adele was love, or something close to that, and not bitterness and hate?

Only time would tell.

And on the subject of time, I had less than three hours until curfew at Mum and Dad's.

I had intended to spend the entire day making Christmas decorations for my business. Instead I'd spent more than an hour with Adele, a few hours here, and then almost an hour with Marcus, counting both times we talked. The first time over the fence and the second inside his cottage.

After that it was back to Adele's for twenty or so minutes and then here, getting soaked by a tap, and then thinking about why I shouldn't be wanting to have sex with a gorgeous, hunky and, I suspected, exceedingly passionate plumber.

So, although I had avoided him as much as possible and shut myself away in the sitting room on the pretext of making my Christmas decorations, all I had really done was stare out of the window, and swoon over Alec.

At least he had fixed my tap. Which meant I could turn that on without risk of a drenching, so I strolled into the kitchen to make a cup of tea, but decided to have a mug of hot chocolate instead.

After heating the milk and mixing it with the mint-flavoured hot chocolate powder, I topped it with whipped cream, added a chocolate flake, some chocolate sprinkles, and a few marshmallows shaped as stars, and dusted those with cocoa powder. It was almost a dessert as well as a hot drink.

I opened one of the bags of Adele's cinnamon biscuits that I'd bought from her that afternoon, having already opened one earlier, to give Alec biscuits with his tea, all of which had been eaten. I'd just have two with my hot chocolate, but I'd take the bag with me, just in case.

By the time I had to leave to get to my parents' house, the second bag was also empty. This cinnamon biscuit addiction was getting serious, and it was only the first day of eating them.

I had intended to drive, having only had one glass of wine with Marcus, but I needed to walk off those biscuits.

It was a bitterly cold evening and I wrapped my scarf around my neck and chin and pulled my bobble hat down further over my ears. My coat was thick and my boots were fleece-lined, as were my leather gloves, so it was only my eyes and nose that were exposed to the elements but when a car honked and pulled up beside me, Berry exploded with laughter.

'Evening, Rudolph,' she teased. 'Will you light our way to the pub, with your bright red nose?'

'Guess who's going on Santa's naughty list,' I parried.

'Hey, Noelle,' said Paul.

I bent slightly to look in at him and remembered why I'd got a crush on him in the first place.

'Hey yourself, Paul.'

'Coming with us?' Berry asked.

'Where to?' I queried.

'The pub, Dumbo.'

'Ah. I believe you're getting your cartoon characters mixed up, but as for the pub, that'd be a firm, no thanks.'

'Why not?'

I frowned at her.

'Because I was drunk on Saturday, not drunk but did drink on Sunday, and I've had a large glass of white wine today. Expensive white wine I might add. That's taken care of my alcohol consumption for the week, I believe. Fourteen units, remember?'

'Who are you and what have you done with my friend, Noelle?'

'Please come,' said Paul, leaning across his sister. 'I'd like to ask you something.'

That made it very tempting, and yet I said no.

'I'm sorry but I really can't tonight. I

need to be at Mum and Dad's before ten or
they'll lock me out. It's nine forty-five-ish
now. I checked just before you pulled up.
Perhaps you could ask me tomorrow?'

'Hop in,' Paul said. 'If you won't come to
the pub, at least let me give you a lift to your
house.'

He didn't have to tell me twice, and I
opened the rear passenger door and climbed
in.

'Thank you so much for this. It's really
cold out there. They forecast snow but I think
it's too cold for that.'

'Whatever,' said Berry, swivelling round
on her seat to look at me. 'Paul wants to ask
you out on a date.'

'Oh!' I shot a look at him and then back
at Berry. Both were smiling. 'Erm. Do you?'

'I do,' he said, nodding.

'Well. That would be lovely. Thank you.'

'See,' said Berry nudging him in the ribs
even though he was driving. 'I told you she
had the hots for you.' And then she grinned
at me. 'I could tell. Although I'm
disappointed you didn't share your feelings
with me. We'll be sisters if this works out.
And I'm sure it will. Imagine that. I'll be
auntie to your kids. All six of them. Paul's
always wanted lots of kids. This is going to be
our best Christmas ever. I can feel it.'

Paul met my eyes in the rearview mirror

and the look he shot me made me feel my entire future had been mapped out by Berry and her brother.

I laughed nervously. 'Erm. Hold on there, tiger. Let's not run before we can walk. And six kids? Really? I'm thirty-six now so that's some going. I've always preferred smaller families.'

'Nah,' said the terrible twosome in unison. That name for them had popped into my head. 'Big families are best.'

As he pulled up outside my parents', Paul jumped out of the car and held the door open for me, sliding his arm around my waist and pulling me close the second I got out.

His face was inches from mine and his hot breath warmed my nose.

'Think of the fun we'll have making those six kids,' he said, his mouth closing in on me as he tugged at my scarf with his fingers. 'I've fancied you since we met. That's why my ex was so mad. I think she knew. I was going to tell her anyway, so don't worry about that. I was going to dump her for you, I just hadn't got around to it yet. Wanna come and stay at my place tonight instead?'

'Erm. Tempting, but no. Thank you. It's been a hectic day. I need my sleep.'

Out of the corner of my eye, I could see Berry leaning across the seat and watching us and I was frozen on the spot, but not from the cold, from irrational fear.

Fear of Berry being our constant companion, fear of six kids, fear of Paul's impending kiss. A kiss I'd been wanting since the first day we'd met.

A kiss that, when it came, wasn't as nice as I'd imagined it would be. In fact, it wasn't that nice at all. It was a sloppy kiss. A cold kiss, if that made sense. A kiss that lacked emotion, and yet his voice, his looks, his body all suggested he wanted me. His kiss told me I might as well have kissed a frog.

Was this how Paul usually kissed? Or were we simply incompatible in the lip-locking department?

I think I might've breathed a sigh of relief when it was over. I definitely felt relieved, and as he came in for another, saying, 'That was nice,' I ducked out of the way and somehow managed to wriggle free of his arm and the body of the car.

'Uh-huh,' I lied. 'I must go in. Good night.'

'Oh. Good night, babe,' Paul said. 'Pleasant dreams. I know what I'll be dreaming about.'

'Night-night,' said Berry, giving me a strange look.

'Good night,' I said forcing a smile.

'I'll give you a bell,' Paul called out.

I assumed he meant he'd phone me, not

that he'd give me an actual bell. Unless he thought I was some sort of prize cow and he was going to hang a bell around my neck.

I had never wanted to get inside my parents' house so fast. And for the first time in my adult life, I genuinely hoped that a man who had told me he would call me – wouldn't.

I called out to Mum and Dad and said I needed the loo, then I rushed upstairs and sent Madi a text.

'Are you free? If so, please call me. If not, don't worry. I'll tell you everything tomorrow.'

A second or two later, Madi called and I told her all about Paul, the odd behaviour, and that kiss.

'Crikey' she said. 'It's weird, isn't it? We build up this image and impression of what a person will be like and all the signs tell us we're right. Then suddenly we discover they're a chameleon and they're not at all the person we thought they were. If anyone other than you had told me all that about Paul, I'd have called them a liar.'

'I know! I don't believe it myself and I was there. Oh god, Madi. What am I going to do?'

'Move to Somerset, I would suggest.'

'That might not be such a bad idea. How could I have been so wrong about a person who seemed so right?'

'Ask Marcus that question. And every other divorced person on the planet. And all the people conned by those romance scammers. Folks just ain't who they make out they are, honey-child.' Madi laughed.

'That's very true. At least I discovered Paul's ... quirks, before our first date. Imagine if I hadn't found out, and we did end up getting married. Although I couldn't take many more of those dreadful kisses, so it wouldn't have got that far.'

'I expect the wedding's booked for next week. He'd want to make a start on those six kids.'

'He wanted to make a start tonight. Thank god my parents not only lock but also bolt the front door.' I laughed.

'At least you can't say your life is boring. I think this is going to be an exciting and eventful Christmas in Fairlight Bay. Why did I have to fall head over hills in love with a man who wanted to live in Somerset, and not one who wanted to live in your neck of the woods?'

'That's a question I often ask. I miss you so much, Madi. I wish you were here. Especially as I've got to face Paul and Berry. I can avoid them until Thursday but I must go to the market stall that day.'

'We'll think of something. Now get some

sleep. You'll need it if you're going to live with six kids and a kissing frog.'

'You're so funny. Good night.'

Thirteen

Once again, Dad gave me a lift home. We'd had a similar discussion over breakfast about why I hadn't arrived in my car, but this time I didn't mention that I'd had alcohol.

'You haven't been banned or something, have you?' Mum asked. 'You have been drinking heavily since you met that Berry person, and her brother.'

'No, Mum. I haven't. I ate rather a lot of my neighbour's delicious cinnamon cookies and I needed to walk off the excess calories. I've brought you a bag, and one for Gran if you're popping into the care home to see her.'

'You're trying to make us fat?' Mum looked horrified.

'No. I'm trying to give you a delicious treat. One a day won't hurt you. I had ... several yesterday.'

'Oh, I see. Well thank you. I'll pass your gift to your gran. But she's not in a care home, darling,' Mum said. 'It's a residential establishment and community for the elderly.'

'Otherwise known as a care home.'

'I'll give you a lift,' said Dad.

It was clearly time to go.

'You won't be coming back, will you?' Mum checked.

'What? Ever?' I asked, knowing full well what she meant.

Mum looked flustered. 'No. Of course not. You'll be here for Sunday lunch. I meant, you won't need to stay tonight, will you? Your plumber is coming to sort you out today, isn't he?'

'Ooooh yes,' I said in as sultry a voice as I could muster. 'I do hope so. My plumbing needs a good sorting out.'

Mum furrowed her brows; Dad quirked one of his.

I didn't bother to tell her he arrived yesterday and was returning today.

'Oh, Lord,' said Dad. 'It's snowing. Hurry up or we won't be able to go anywhere.'

I dashed to the front door and flung it open. A solitary snowflake landed on my nose.

'We might need to dig our way out, Dad,' I said.

Dad shook his head and walked past me.

'You don't have to wind your mother up,' Dad said once we'd left the driveway.

'I know. But I can't help myself.'

'Try,' he said.

I threw him a look. 'Okay. But I make no promises.'

'Just do your best. That's all I ask. That's all we've ever asked.'

'Do you and Mum love me, Dad?'

He almost drove onto the pavement. He coughed, and puffed out his cheeks. He glanced in the rearview mirror and his fingers tightened on the steering wheel.

'What sort of a question is that? Of course we do. It goes without saying.'

'No it doesn't. Gran often says it.'

'Your grandmother has dementia.'

'Ah. Is that why she says it? I thought it was because she cared about me.' I knew Gran loved me. She loved me a lot.

'She does. We all do. And we know you love us all, in your own little way.'

I almost burst out laughing.

'My own little way? Yes, Dad. I do.' Now the snow was coming down a little harder and faster. 'You can drop me here. I'd hate you to get stuck in a snow drift on Midwinter Ridge.' It wasn't settling yet so there was no chance of that.

'Good point. Your mother hates being left in the house for too long on her own.'

He pulled the car over and I quickly got out.

'Thanks, Dad. See you soon. Drive safely.'

'I always drive safely. You're the one who needs to do that.'

'I love you too,' I said as he drove off.

Then like a kid of five, I stuck my thumbs in my ears and waggled my fingers at his car while sticking out my tongue. I just couldn't help myself.

I noticed the van drive by and stop a few feet ahead but I didn't think anything of it until I walked past and a deep gravelly voice said good morning.

I stopped but took a step away. Just in case. I reached my black belt in karate but it'd been years since I'd used it. My karate, not the black belt itself.

Alec beamed at me from the van. 'Let me guess. That was your blind date. I take it things went well if you spent the night. But why did he drop you off here? Oh wait. You're not that sort of girl, are you?'

'Go and fix a pipe or something.'

'I'm on my way to fix yours. But tell me, why did you step away from my van? Don't you trust yourself to be near me?'

I glowered at him.

'I didn't know it was you. If I had, I'd have crossed the road to avoid you and your sarcasm. For all I knew, you could've been a murderer. Or someone who was going to kidnap me.'

'Because that happens a lot in Fairlight Bay.'

'It happens everywhere. You hear about things like that on the news.'

'I rarely listen to the news.'

'Why doesn't that surprise me? How did you know it was me, anyway? Or do you pick up your dates from the streets?'

'No, I don't. I collect them from their homes and I take them back to their homes afterwards. I'd recognise you anywhere. Even with your clothes on.'

I narrowed my eyes at him and he grinned.

'Has anyone ever told you you're a pain in the arse?'

'Frequently. But I'm also a lot of fun. And I'm kind, and thoughtful, and I can be romantic. With the right woman.'

'Tell someone who gives a damn.'

'I thought I was. Get in.'

'Don't tell me what to do!'

'Fine. Would you like a lift? I'm going to your cottage anyway, so it's really no trouble.'

I hesitated for a moment and he laughed.

'What's funny now?' I hissed.

'You are. Are you seriously going to stand there and think about it? It's snowing and it's freezing. I promise I'm not going to murder you. Or kidnap you. Or do anything else to you. Unless you want me to do something to you, of course. Then I'd be only too happy to oblige.'

I gasped.

'All I want you to do is to fix my heating.'

'Then the sooner you stop acting like an idiot and get in, the sooner I can get that done.'

'An idiot? You're calling me an idiot?'

'If the shoe fits, wear it. As I've said before. I'm busy at this time of year.'

'Hmm. Picking up women from the street, I bet.' I mumbled as I walked around and got in the passenger side.

He grinned at me as he let off the handbrake. 'Well it worked with you, didn't it?'

I glared at him in silence, all the way to Midwinter Lane, which was at least a five-minute drive.

'Any chance of a coffee?' he asked when he parked.

'You know where it is. Help yourself.'

'I'm charging you by the hour, you do know that, don't you?'

'It takes three minutes to make a cup of coffee. I can afford that. I'm not your personal waitress.'

He sighed and got out. 'Fine. Do you want one?'

'What?'

'If I'm making coffee anyway, I may as well make one for you.'

'Look. I don't know what you think is happening here, and I know I need you far more than you need me, but if you're trying it on with me, you can forget it. I admit we had ... a moment yesterday, but that's all it was. A moment. And it was a ... strange situation. You stay away from me and I'll stay away from you and then nothing like that will happen again.'

I marched off as he grabbed his tools but he had caught up with me within seconds and we walked across the bridge together. Annoyingly, I slipped on the snow that was now settling, here on Midwinter Ridge, and he caught me in his arms, dropping his tool bag onto the bridge to do so.

'I've got you,' he said in a tone that made my insides turn to mush.

'Thanks. You can let me go now.'

'Must I?'

Our eyes met and held as snowflakes danced around us.

'Yes,' I said. 'You must.'

'Fine. Just let me say this first. I have no idea what's happening here either. I didn't want this or expect this anymore than you did, and I don't know what this is. But you're right. We did have a moment yesterday. And it was more than a moment for me. In fact, I can't stop thinking about it. Or about you. I'm not trying it on with you, believe me. My circumstances are such that I can't start a relationship right now. However much I might want to. Sex is sex and if it's just for fun, that's fine. But I think with you, it would be more than just sex. For me, at least. So I agree we need to make sure it doesn't happen again. But do we really have to avoid one another? We're both adults, aren't we? We might be tempted to do something we shouldn't but does that mean we will? I have self-control. And, if this morning is anything to go by, you now have a boyfriend.'

'You ... you're wrong. That was my dad. I don't have a boyfriend. Although someone did ask me out last night. But that's another story. As for self-control. I have that too. And I agree, sex is fine if it's just fun, but not if someone is already with a relationship with someone else. So yes. We'll both behave like grown ups and we should be fine. And I'll make the coffee. You get on with the job. That's why you're here, after all.'

I got my footing and gingerly walked on. He picked up his tool bag and caught up with me.

'That is why I'm here,' he said. 'Although you are wrong too. About you needing me far more than I need you. I know you meant as a plumber and a client but I mean it in a personal way. But we won't take that any further.'

I looked at him open-mouthed, as we strode up my garden path, until Adele and Marcus tumbled out of Adele's cottage, arm-in-arm, kissing as they did so, right in front of our eyes.

Marcus coughed loudly and smiled and nodded as they pulled away from one another, both red-faced, flushed with happiness, and with love in their eyes.

'All right?' Alec said.

'Yeah. Great,' said Marcus. 'You?'

'Not bad.'

Marcus glanced at me. 'Hello, Noelle,'

No words would come out so I smiled and nodded.

'Erm. You remember Adele, Alec?' Marcus pulled her closer.

'Yes. Hi Adele. You okay?'

'Hi Alec. I'm more than okay, thanks. Hello, Noelle. I'll be in with you soon to start work.'

Marcus smiled at her lovingly as I watched on in silent disbelief, but also thrilled to bits.

'Uh-huh,' I nodded and quickly unlocked my front door.

'See you later,' Alec said, following me inside and grinning at me as I closed the door behind us.

'Do you always have so much to say when you bump into your neighbours?'

'Drop the sarcasm. I was surprised. Okay? Those two haven't spoken one word to one another for almost two years and now look at them?'

'I'm aware of that. And I was looking at them. I haven't seen Marcus this happy in years. I didn't know Adele that well because my wife and I had other friends we hung out with more than Marcus and his mates in those days, but I always thought she was nice. And I didn't believe any of that crap Cara said about her.'

'Your wife?'

I don't know why I was surprised by that. I knew he was married or something from that phone call yesterday, but suddenly everything he'd said and done on that bridge just now came back and slapped me in the face like a massive and rock-solid ball of ice.

'My wife?' He furrowed his brows. 'Why has that surprised you? Marcus told you my situation.'

'Marcus told me nothing. I didn't even know he'd called you, remember? But how dare you say all those things and make me feel the way you do! And yesterday, if I'd dropped that towel and laid down on my bed, you'd have had sex with me, wouldn't you?'

'Yes. No. I ... I don't know, to be honest.

Were you … were you considering dropping that towel? Because believe me I was hoping you would. Even though I wasn't sure what I'd do if you did.'

'You're unbelievable! And you just told me you weren't trying it on with me! You're nothing but a liar.'

He glowered at me. 'I am many things, but a liar is not one of them. I haven't lied to you. I've actually been more open and honest with you than I have with any woman over the last five years.'

'Five years? You've been seeing other women for five years?'

'No. I only started seeing other women about three years ago. But I've never felt anything for any of them like I felt for you yesterday. And I feel for you today, if I'm being honest. Which I am. I've told you how I'm feeling, and that's pretty terrifying for me.'

'I bet it is. You're really something. Make your own coffee. I'm going for a walk. Call me when you're done and I'll pay you. And then I never want to see you again.'

'What? Why? What have I done now? Talk to me, Noelle.'

'No. Talk to yourself.'

I stormed off leaving Alec looking utterly dumbfounded and scratching his head as if he had no clue what had just happened.

Obviously, the moment I got outside, I phoned Madi and regaled her with the whole sorry tale.

'What a jerk,' she said. 'Stay away from the man.'

'I intend to. I certainly know how to pick them, don't I? Oh, but at least two other people are happy.'

I told her about Adele and Marcus.

'Crikey. They didn't waste any time did they?'

'They wasted the last two years. And even longer, if you take into account that if he had asked her out when he wanted to all those years earlier, none of that stuff with Cara and Jeff would ever have happened.'

'True. It's all about timing, isn't it? And maybe being in the right place at the right time.'

'Or in my case, the wrong place at the wrong time. I'm sorry I keep calling you, Madi, but it's feels as if my life is spiralling out of control. Even the snow which seemed to be dancing around me and Alec on the bridge, is now twirling around me, relentlessly. It appears to be making fun of me.'

'Yeah. Because snow does that, of course. Call me later with an update. Or even if you just need to chat. I'm always here for you, Noelle. You know that.'

'Love you,' I said.

'Love you too.'

I rang off and the snow twirled even more.

'You are such a fool, Noelle,' it seemed to be saying.

Or perhaps that was me, talking to myself.

Fourteen

I couldn't believe it was Thursday already. I had no idea where Wednesday went. I spent most of it wallowing in self-pity and watching the small amount of snow that had settled, melt. It was ironic that Marcus and Adele were now blissfully happy, and I was the one down in the dumps.

They had even put up decorations inside and outside of both of their cottages. They had invited me to join in, but now I was the grinch who ignored the invitations.

Well, I didn't ignore them. I simply said no and that I wasn't feeling well.

Tuesday had been an awful day after that row with Alec. The less said about that the better. But he did fix my heating and had replaced the timer and of course, he'd already mended the tap. So everything in the cottage was running perfectly.

Apart from me.

He had left me a note saying that he was

sorry if he'd done anything to upset me as that was the last thing he wanted to do. And he hoped that we would meet again when things might be different.

Jerk.

He had charged me for the timer, but he'd thrown in the tap for free. I paid his bill immediately, and didn't respond to his prompt payment thank you email that arrived the same day.

I had popped into Adele's after speaking to Madi, rather than Adele coming to me as agreed. I explained that I was juggling some personal issues and asked if we could bake cookies instead of making Christmas decorations.

She didn't seem to pick up on my low mood but she was so joyful about her own new love life, who could blame her?

She told me how Marcus had arrived at her door, more than a little tipsy, and how he had apologised profusely, and told her she had been right about Cara and Jeff all along. She said they had talked all evening and for most of the night and then something had changed between them.

Marcus had taken her hands in his and said, 'I should've married you, Adele, not Cara. I should've asked you out when I had intended to and not listened to Jeff. I should've trusted my owns feelings. So I'm trusting them now. I think, deep down, I've always loved you. I know I said and did some horrible things, but all I can say is I was a total idiot. Noelle has helped to open my eyes and see what's in front of me. I don't deserve your forgiveness, and I'm definitely not worthy of your love, but I sincerely hope you'll forgive me, and if you'll give me a chance, I'll spend the rest of my days showing you how much you mean to me. I love you, Adele. Is there any chance you'd consider going out with me?'

Adele said she couldn't speak because she was so surprised. Never in her wildest dreams could she have imagined Marcus might love her. But she eventually managed to nod and say yes.

And then, like the woman in love she really was, she had grabbed Marcus by his shirt collar and planted a kiss on his lips.

'You should've seen his face, Noelle. One minute it was all contrition and heartfelt honesty. The next it was pure love and passion. He kissed me back and then he pulled me into his arms and we kissed, and kissed, and kissed. I think we might've kissed all night if I hadn't told him to take me to bed and make love to me. He honestly looked like a child who had got every toy on his Christmas wish-list, and a special bonus toy on top.'

'I'm so happy for you both,' I said. 'I was hoping we might all become friends by Christmas and that maybe at some stage, you two might develop that friendship into something more. This is beyond even my wildest dreams.'

'And mine,' she said. 'And I believe we owe it all to you.'

'You owe me nothing. All I did was move into Middle Cottage and hope I could persuade my neighbours to put up some Christmas decorations. You two did all the rest yourselves. All three cottages now look so festive, I'm the one who should be thanking you.'

Despite my own broken heart; and as ridiculous as that might be, it did feel as though Alec had broken my heart with those two little words – my wife; I had a lovely time with Adele. And I ate far too many cinnamon cookies. But I'm allowed. That's what you do with heartbreak.

All I wanted to do on Wednesday was stay curled up in bed, and I'd have done the same on Thursday if I could. But I had to be at the market stall on Thursday. And that meant a new can of worms.

Paul had texted me and phoned me twice. I had replied by text saying I was unwell. Berry texted to see if I needed anything, but I said I didn't, and thanked her.

I couldn't leave this any longer though. I'd have to tell them I had changed my mind about dating Paul.

I dressed in my favourite black trousers, and wore a sparkly, glittery, Christmas jumper with a Christmas tree on it that lit up. I wore Christmas tree shaped earrings to match, and I put on some make up to help myself feel more human and less like death warmed up.

I arrived at the market stall at eight on the dot and Berry came over right away. Our stalls weren't together today. Her stall was a few stalls away and there was a stall selling Christmas spiced punch, mulled wine and other festive drinks; one selling mince pies, Christmas puddings and Christmas cakes, and another selling handmade Christmas stockings.

Fortunately, several customers arrived at my stall before I'd finished displaying my stock and I told Berry we'd have to chat later.

The morning flew and by lunchtime the market was packed. But I spotted a face I recognised in the crowd, and Marcus, having spotted me, came over to chat while there was a lull in my sales, as everyone made beelines for food and drink stalls.

'I'm glad things worked out with you and Adele,' I said.

He beamed at me. 'Me too. I owe you

more than I'll ever be able to repay.'

'No you don't. I still owe you for those wines.'

'Nope. I'm in your debt,' he laughed. 'Seriously, Noelle. I had thought this was going to be another awful Christmas. Now it's going to be my best Christmas ever. And that's all thanks to you.'

I saw someone approaching and panic set in.

'I meant what I said. You owe me nothing. But ... I know this is a huge thing to ask and I wouldn't, except I'm desperate. Would you kiss me, Marcus? Please? Right now. No questions. I'll explain later and I'll tell Adele.'

His face was a picture of astonishment. 'Oh. Erm. I don't know. Cheating isn't something I do.'

'It's not cheating. It's just a kiss for a friend. A friend in dire need. And it's an emergency. There's no one else I can ask.'

'Erm.'

'P-lease! I'm begging you. Just put your arms around me and give me a kiss.'

He took a deep breath. 'If this causes a problem with Adele, I'll never forgive you.'

'It won't. I promise. She'll understand when I explain. Two seconds left to help me.'

'Fine.'

I flung my arms around him and he

wrapped his around me and we kissed. But our lips hardly touched and neither of us made any effort.

I peered over his shoulder and when I was sure it was safe, I whispered. 'You can stop now.'

He stopped immediately and we stepped away from one another. Paul and Berry stood open mouthed just a few feet away.

'Oh no,' I said, linking my arm through Marcus'. 'I'm so sorry you had to see that. I wanted to tell you both before you found out. The thing is. I've fallen for someone else. He's been looking after me, and well, you know how it is. These things happen. Love moves in mysterious ways. I hope we can still be friends.'

I could see Marcus looked as astonished as Berry and Paul, who both turned on their heels and marched away.

Perhaps this had been a mistake after all. What on earth had possessed me to think this was a good idea? But it was the only thing I could think of that would ensure Paul didn't ask me out. The prospect of explaining that I no longer fancied him had filled me with dread, but I hadn't thought this through. I might lose Berry's friendship over this. I'd probably lose Paul's. Why had I been so crazy?

'Explain, please,' said Marcus in a low

voice, still looking a little shell shocked.

'Give me a minute and I'll try,' I whispered.

'Love moves in mysterious ways, does it?'

I recognised the gravelly voice instantly and spun around to see Alec standing behind me.

'What are you doing here?' I asked, annoyed that he'd seen and heard all that.

'I came for some Christmas treats. I see Marcus did the same.' He gave Marcus a cold, hard stare as he did me.

'It wasn't what you think,' said Marcus. 'Noelle was desperate.'

'Was she indeed?' His raised brows said more than his sarcasm could.

'We're not in love,' Marcus added. 'We're just friends. Say something, Noelle.'

'Why do we need to explain to him? He's hardly in a position to cast stones.'

'What?' Marcus looked even more confused.

'I never thought I'd see the day when you would cheat on a woman, Marcus,' said Alec.

'I wasn't!'

'Kissing another woman is cheating,' Alec said.

'I wasn't kissing her. Not really! Please, Noelle explain this to him and to me.'

'I was trying to stop a man from asking

me out, and all I could think of on the spur of the moment, and because Marcus happened to be here at just the right time, was that if the man saw me kissing someone else, he wouldn't want me as his girlfriend.'

'I agree with that,' Alec said, looking me up and down as if even the dog wouldn't drag me in. 'I may be out of practice regarding dating but surely you could've simply told this other man that you didn't want to date him?'

'I suppose I could've. But it isn't that simple. You don't know the man, or the situation.'

He raised his brows once again. 'I know that most people just say, 'no thanks', if they don't want to go out with someone. And I also know that if two people kiss, it usually means it's because they want to.'

'Marcus didn't want to kiss me. I made him. He wasn't cheating. It was all me, okay? I told him I needed him to kiss me, and like the friend that he is, he helped me when I needed him to do so. If I'd seen you, I might've asked you to kiss me instead.'

'Damn. If only I'd known, I wouldn't have spent so long buying that quilt for my mum. I'd have hurried over here to kiss you.'

'Sarcasm is the lowest form of wit.'

'And cheating is the lowest form of relationship.'

I gasped at that. 'People in glass houses and all that.'

'What's going on here?' Marcus asked.

'This so-called friend of yours would've had sex with me if I'd dropped my towel in my bedroom the other day and he has the nerve to tell us that you and I are in the wrong. Unlike you, Alec, neither of us has a wife.'

Alec and Marcus exchanged confused glances.

'None of us are married,' Marcus said.

'He is.' I pointed at Alec and he looked around, as did Marcus.

'Are you pointing at me?' Alec asked.

'Yes. Of course I am.'

'Why?' asked Marcus. 'Alec doesn't have a wife. At least. Not now.'

'Oh. Erm. Wait. Don't tell me. She left because of his cheating. You told me yourself you had a wife.'

'Yes. I did. Several years ago. But she didn't leave me because I cheated. I have never cheated on anyone in my life. My wife died almost six years ago now.'

'Daddy! Daddy! Look what Granddad bought me.'

The most beautiful little girl who resembled Alec in so many ways, grabbed his hand and waggled it.

'Show me, sweetheart,' he said, in a soft

and loving voice as he dragged his eyes from my now bright red face and smiled adoringly down at her.

And then he swept her up in his strong arms as she held out a little reindeer Christmas ornament.

One of my reindeer Christmas ornaments.

One I'd sold to this little girl and her granddad just half an hour or so earlier.

We'd chatted about how much she loved reindeer, and that her daddy was joining them at the market later, and that next year he was taking her to see real reindeer in Norway and they would stay in a hotel made of ice, and would visit Santa and his elves, and take a sleigh ride with huskies, and see some pretty lights in the night sky.

And suddenly all the Christmas bells on the planet clanged loudly in my head.

This was the person he had spoken to that day in my kitchen.

She was the reason he couldn't start a relationship right now.

He was no doubt spending all his free time in December concentrating on making her Christmas special and planning their trip for next year.

And I was the biggest idiot this side of Mars.

'This nice lady sold it to me,' the little girl

said.

'Did she? That's lovely.' He didn't look at me. 'Let's go and get some hot chocolate?' He smiled over her to her granddad who smiled and nodded at me.

'That sounds good, doesn't it? If you want to stay and chat to your friends, Alec, I can take Melody, and you can meet us there.'

'No. It's okay, thanks. I'm done here. Bye, Marcus. Bye, Noelle. Merry Christmas to you both. And to Adele.'

Merry Christmas,' Alec's daughter said to me.

And then Alec turned and walked out of my life, carrying his beautiful little girl whom he clearly adored.

'Kill me now,' I said.

'You thought he was married?' Marcus queried. 'I told you his wife was dead.'

'When?'

'On Monday when we had that drink together and I said I had a friend who was perfect for you.'

'Alec was that friend?'

'Of course. You said you didn't want to go on a blind date, but when you told me about your boiler, I thought it was the perfect way for the two of you to meet. And then if you both saw what I saw, you'd fall for one another in a more natural and casual way.'

'Why did I do that? I'm such an idiot!' I

said. 'He hates me.'

'I think that's a bit strong, but he does seem to be a little disappointed in you. And in me. If Adele reacts in the same way, you will be dead, because I'll kill you myself.'

Fifteen

Fortunately for both me and Marcus, although Adele wasn't thrilled with me kissing her new boyfriend, she did seem to understand why I'd done it.

'Perhaps you could explain it to me then,' I said with a sheepish smile. 'I don't know what I was thinking, and if I could go back in time and do it again, I wouldn't. I'd just tell Paul I'd changed my mind and I didn't want to go out with him.'

'That would've been much simpler,' said Adele. 'But love makes us do strange things.'

'Love? I'm not in love.'

She and Marcus exchanged looks. We were having drinks and supper in Marcus' cottage, on Thursday evening, after the market had closed, and he opened more of that exquisite wine.

'I think you are,' she said. 'I know what unrequited love feels like and I recognise the symptoms.'

'I knew you two would fall for one another,' said Marcus. 'It's odd how we can often see why others would make a perfect couple but when it comes to ourselves, we rarely see what's right in front of our nose.'

'There's no chance of Alec and me being a couple now. But I don't know why he didn't simply tell me about his dead wife.'

'Maybe for the same silly reason you didn't simply tell Paul you weren't interested. He wasn't thinking straight.'

'He thought you knew,' said Marcus. 'If he speaks to me again, which I believe he will because I've already sent him an email explaining, and Adele has signed it saying she's fine with what happened, I'll tell him once more that you had no knowledge of his marital status. I have put that in the email but it's not the same as saying something face to face.'

'Thanks, Marcus. You're a good friend.'

'Just don't ask me to kiss you ever again,' He threw me an amused stare.

'No, don't,' said Adele.

'I promise I won't. But could I ask you both to help me with my Christmas tree, please? The one for the sitting room. I'm having it delivered tomorrow but I'm not feeling as festive as I should and I could do with some company while I'm decorating it. I know I didn't help you, and I'm sorry. This is selfish, I know.'

'We'll gladly help,' said Marcus.

'And I'll bake some cinnamon cookies,' said Adele.

'I'll bring wine,' added Marcus. 'I could invite Alec and see if he'll come. I could say Melody is welcome.'

'No. I think he needs some time to see how he feels,' I said. 'And to see that you and Adele are fine, and that we're all still friends.'

I didn't think I'd see Alec again for a while – if at all, so you can imagine my surprise when I saw him on Saturday at the Fairlight Bay Christmas Market.

I was feeling happier and more festive having put the Christmas tree up in my sitting room on Friday with help from Adele and Marcus. We'd played Christmas music, and sang along with all the songs we knew. We'd eaten festive treats like Adele's cinnamon cookies and some of my own Christmas cookies, plus sausage rolls, mince pies, chocolate log, and various festive-themed cheeses. We'd drunk Marcus' wine, as well as some port with the cheeses, and that might have added to my mellow feeling on Saturday morning.

I'd taken photos of the finished tree on Friday, and all the decorations on the outside of all three cottages, and sent them to Madi, and she'd sent several photos of the decorations at Apple Orchard Farm. It was as beautiful this year as it had been last year.

The cottages on Midwinter Lane looked truly sensational this year, now that Adele and Marcus had gone to great lengths to make their cottages both as bright and as Christmassy as possible. Adele might have been struggling financially but both myself and Marcus gave her decorations to put up on Far Cottage, and once the local authority had also hung festive wreaths on the lampposts on the lane, this part of Midwinter Ridge was warm and bright and beautiful.

I was ensuring my display of Christmas decorations on my stall at the Fairlight Bay Christmas Market was as welcoming and enticing to shoppers as I could possibly make it, when Alec's daughter, Melody came bounding up to my stall. I recognised her immediately.

'Hello, again,' I said looking around for her dad, who was nowhere to be seen. 'Who are you here with today?'

'Daddy's friend. You look pretty. Are those earrings for sale?' She was pointing to my dancing reindeer earrings.

'Yes. There's a stall in this market that sells them. I'm not sure where it is today but it will definitely be here somewhere. Who's your daddy's friend? And where are they?'

She spun around on the spot and held

her arm aloft waving her hand as if she were holding a wand.

'Erm ... Somewhere.' She shrugged. 'We were walking towards your stall and she said she wanted to stop and look at some pretty soaps and that I should look too. But I wanted to come and see your Christmas decorations.'

'She? Your daddy's friend is a woman?'

'Uh-huh. But she's not as pretty as you.' She tipped her head to one side. 'What's the difference between a friend and a special friend?' She picked up another reindeer decoration and hugged it to her. 'This is so pretty. I'm going to ask if I can have it.'

'A friend and a special friend? Well, a friend is someone a person knows and likes. A special friend is someone that person likes a lot. Like a best friend. Or a girlfriend. Why do you ask? Is this woman a special friend of your daddy's?'

'Oh no!' She shook her head vehemently. 'She's a friend Daddy pays to look after me when he's working and when Nanna and Granddad can't.'

I breathed a sigh of relief. 'Oh. A baby sitter, you mean?' She glowered at me and I added hastily, 'No. Not a baby sitter. You're not a baby, are you? You're a young lady. So she's your friend too.'

Melody shrugged. 'A friend, yes. But not

a special friend.'

'Does your daddy have any special friends?'

Okay. I know I shouldn't have been putting his daughter through an inquisition, but how else was I going to find out?

Again she shook her head. 'No. Not at the moment. He said he thought you might be a special friend when he told me about you on Monday, but now he says he was mistaken.'

Out of the mouths of babes, as the saying goes.

But at least he'd told her about me.

'What did he say about me?'

She looked up and met my eyes as if she knew I was asking something that she probably shouldn't tell me.

'You can have that reindeer decoration for free, if you tell me. It'll be our little secret.'

Had it come to this? I'd resorted to bribing a child. Were there any depths I wouldn't sink to?

She beamed at me. 'Truly?'

'Yes.'

She leant forward and so did I.

'He said that he'd met a very pretty lady that he liked, and that he was hoping she might become a special friend, and he asked how I would feel if he asked her to join us for ice skating next week when the ice rink opens. I said that would be nice.'

'For skating? That would be nice. How do you know he was talking about me?'

'He said the lady's name was Noelle. Your name is Noelle. I've never met a Noelle before. Would you like me to tell you why he thinks he was mistaken?'

She had popped the reindeer decoration in her little rucksack, and now she was fiddling with another reindeer one. This kid was smart. I might be being played.

'If you want to.'

She met my eyes and hugged the second reindeer. I smiled and waited and she eventually let out a sigh. Kids can't keep secrets. I knew she wanted to tell me.

'It was on Tuesday. He wasn't as happy as he was on Monday and when I asked why he was sad, he said it was grown up stuff but nothing for me to worry about.'

She kissed the reindeer and made a little face. I remained silent and she gave an even bigger sigh.

'Then when I asked if his special friend might want to come to the tree lighting with us next Saturday, he said that he was mistaken about her and that she might not be a special friend after all.'

She placed the reindeer gently back on the table as if she knew she'd lost her leverage.

'You can have that one for free too. But don't tell your dad, okay?'

She nodded madly and her smile was huge. 'Thank you, Noelle. I won't say a word. Bye-ee.'

'Bye, Melody. Wait. Let me take you back to your … friend. You shouldn't be running around here on your own.'

I walked her back to Berry's stall and Melody pointed the woman out.

'I think you might've lost someone,' I said.

The woman gave me an odd look and then glanced at Melody and shrugged.

'Don't wander off again, okay,' I said to Melody. 'Your dad would be worried if he knew. Promise me, Melody.'

'Okay. I promise. Thank you for my reindeer.'

'You're welcome.'

I really liked that kid.

I spent the day feeling depressed that I was no longer considered suitable to be Alec's special friend, and that I'd missed out on what might've been a wonderfully romantic Christmas Tree Lighting Ceremony next Saturday, and also an equally romantic evening skating on the ice with Alec holding my hand and Melody holding his.

I was packing up the few remaining Christmas decorations when I heard Alec's voice.

'Don't ever ask my daughter to tell you how I feel about you. If you want to know how I feel, ask me, not my eight-year-old child.' He threw a twenty pound note on the table. 'And never, ever try to bribe her to do that. She is not a pawn to be toyed with. Or a monkey you can get to dance for you. Or a man to kiss you, when you want to be kissed because you don't have the decency to tell some guy you no longer fancy him. I thought you were special. I was very much mistaken.'

'I didn't bribe her. She was the one who … never mind. Melody is lovely and bright and smart and I really like her. I gave her those reindeer decorations because I wanted to. Not because of anything she may or may not have told me. So keep your bloody money.' I stuffed it in his hand. 'I know I'm not deemed to be worthy to be your special friend, but I would've made a better job of looking after Melody than that woman did today. She was looking at stuff on a stall way over there and Melody came running over to me all on her own. So I'm not the only one you've made a mistake about.'

'She did what?' He gave me a quelling look.

'Buy me a drink and I'll tell you. That was a joke.'

'Really?' His mouth twitched at one

corner.

'Yes. The woman told Melody to stop at the other stall with her but Melody wanted to come here, so she did. She has a mind of her own. But the woman didn't check to see where Melody was. And to be honest, she didn't seem bothered when I took Melody back and told the woman she had lost her.'

'You … you took her back to Clare?'

'If that's her name then yes. Of course I did.'

'Then thank you for that. I owe you an apology.'

'You owe me nothing. Go and find yourself another special friend.'

'Don't get mad with me. You're the one who got the wrong end of the stick. And you're the one who kisses guys to make other guys jealous.'

'I didn't do that. I did it to stop him asking me out. I thought it was the best thing to do. But I accept it was stupid and I was wrong. In my defence, it's been a weird and rather emotional few days. How was I to know your wife was dead? No one told me. You didn't tell me. I'm not a bloody mind reader. I heard you on the phone calling someone sweetheart, and yes, I jumped to conclusions and assumed you weren't single and that you were just trying to get me into bed or something. And how was I to know I'd fall head over heels for you despite the fact you're a pain in the arse and sarcastic and ... and ... far too gorgeous and sexy. Now leave me alone so that I can go home and get drunk. And yes, I drink. Add that to the list of why I'm unsuitable to be your special friend.'

I thought he'd leave, but he didn't. He stood his ground and stared at me for what seemed like an eternity as I packed up my boxes.

'Need a hand with that?'

'Nope. I've got it. Why are you still here?'

'The truth? I'm not sure. I came here to tell you to stay away from my daughter, but it seems my daughter is as drawn to you as I am.'

'Your daughter is drawn to my reindeer decorations, not me.'

'Nope. I found those in her rucksack when I was looking for her hat. I asked her why she had them and she said you'd given them to her. I was cross because I didn't know why you'd done that. And then she asked me why you couldn't be my special friend and that she'd love it if you could be And I got angry. I thought ... well, I'm not sure what I thought. I asked why she wanted you to be my special friend and she said it was because she likes you a lot and that you're pretty and you talk to her more than

Clara does.'

'As I said before, I really like her too. Melody not Clara. I'll stay away from Melody though if that's what you want.'

'I'm not sure what I want. That's not entirely true. I know what I want but I'm not sure it's wise. Yet, there's something about you that's hard to resist. Since the first time I saw you, I've felt drawn to you. As angry as I was on Thursday, I still couldn't stop thinking about you. I haven't stopped thinking about you all week.'

'Well, I'm sorry about that.'

'Don't be. I like having you on my mind. But is this real? Can I trust how I feel? I can't make a mistake. I've got Melody to think about.'

'You're not making any sense. First you come down here and yell at me and then you tell me you ... well, it sounds as if you want to ask me out.'

'What can I say? You make me mad. You make me happy. You've made me feel things I never thought I'd feel again. And I think we both know I want to take you to bed. I think you want me as much as I want you. I'm pretty sure you do. But is this lust? Or is this ... more?'

'Don't ask me. I'm the woman who makes stupid decisions. So I'd say the only way to find out, is to try it and see.'

'Don't just stand there, mate,' a passer-by said, nudging Alec on the arm. 'Kiss the woman. Look up.' He pointed upwards and winked and we both spotted the mistletoe hanging above our heads from a wire crisscrossing the market.

Alec looked me in the eye and a devastating smile spread across his gorgeous mouth.

'I don't think either of us can argue with that. It's tradition, after all.'

'It's bad luck not to. I'd rather not have any more of that, thanks. My boiler played up and so did my tap, and everything comes in threes, so I'd rather kiss you than take a chance on something else going wrong or breaking down.'

'Thanks. I suppose fending off bad luck is as good a reason to kiss me, as doing so to stop someone asking you out. Who would you kiss to stop me asking you out, just out of interest?'

'No one. Because I'd rather like you to ask me out. But then I do make stupid decisions.'

He reached out a hand and took one of mine in his.

'By the way, I know a good plumber if you do have anything else break down.'

'Good. Because the last one left me in a bit of a mess. Personally speaking.'

He took my other hand in his.

'I came here to shout at you, not to kiss you. How did we end up here?'

'I don't have a clue. But I know where I'd like us to end up.'

He smiled again. 'Me too.'

And then he pulled me in close and looked deep into my eyes.

'I can't make any promises other than I don't cheat and I'm not looking for a fling. But I've never felt this way about anyone before, not even my wife and I loved her deeply. If this is going where I hope it is, I'll be in this for life. I need to know if you feel the same. And more importantly, if you're prepared to love Melody as if she were your own child. Because we come as a package and that'll never change.'

'I don't cheat either, but I have made some silly mistakes and jumped to conclusions. I want a family. I want to love someone with all my heart and for them to feel the same about me. As for Melody, I already love her, I think. I may even like her a teensy bit more than I like you, sometimes.'

'That's understandable, Melody's easy to like. I can be hard work.'

'Oh so can I. Just ask my mum.'

We gazed at one another.

'I'm scared,' he said. 'I've never been scared before. It's been a while since I've kissed anyone and I don't want to screw this up.'

'I'm scared too.' I was remembering that awful kiss with Paul. 'I don't want to screw this up either.'

'I suppose one of us will have to make the first move, and I guess that should be me.'

'How very macho of you. I'm happy to take the lead if you don't think you're up to it.'

'Oh, I'm up to it.'

'Are you sure? Because I can imagine how stressful it must be to be so handsome and sexy and for everyone to have such high expectations of you.'

'You've got high expectations? How high?'

'At least a fifteen.'

'Out of twenty? That's not high.'

'Out of ten. Now shut up and kiss me. Because until you do that we can't move onto the next bit.'

His mouth hovered just an inch or two from mine.

'The next bit? What's that?'

I ran a hand inside his coat and let my hand trail up his back. His muscles tensed beneath my touch.

'I believe I have a problem with the shower in the ensuite in my bedroom.'

'Oh really? What's wrong? Wait. If you

knew that you wouldn't need me.'

'Oh I need you. Because you're the problem. You're not in my bedroom. And you should be.'

His mouth was on mine in a second and his kiss was like nothing I'd experienced before. It was deep and passionate and it seemed to reach right into my soul. This was a kiss to die for. This was a kiss to make me feel that all the heavens and the entire universe existed just so that we could share this kiss. This was a kiss I wanted to experience over and over again for the rest of my life.

And from the way Alec was reacting, I was pretty certain, he felt the same.

This was going to be the best Christmas ever. And I couldn't wait to spend it with Alec and with Melody.

I didn't even care what Mum and Dad might say. But I knew Gran would be thrilled.

And I couldn't wait to tell Madi. Although ... maybe I'd just send her a very quick text and tell her I'd call her tomorrow.

I had a gorgeous man to make love with.

And that was going to keep us both occupied for some considerable time.

Coming soon

Visit www.emilyharvale.com to
see what's coming next.

Plus, sign up for Emily's newsletter, or
join her Facebook group, for all the latest
news about her books.

Stay in touch with

Emily Harvale

If you want to be the first to hear Emily's news, find out about book releases, see covers and maybe chat with other fans, there are a few options for you:

visit: www.emilyharvale.com

Or join her Facebook group for all of the above and to chat with others about her books:

www.emilyharvale.com/FacebookGroup

Alternatively, just come and say 'Hello' on social media:

 @EmilyHarvaleWriter

 @EmilyHarvale

 @EmilyHarvale

A Note from Emily

Thank you for reading this book. I really hope it brought a smile to your face. If so, I'd love it if you'd leave a short review on Amazon, or even just a rating.
And, maybe, tell your friends, or mention it on social media.

A little piece of my heart goes into all my books. I can't wait to bring you more stories that I hope will capture your heart, mind and imagination, allowing you to escape into a world of romance in some enticingly beautiful settings.

To see my books, or to sign up for my newsletter, please visit my website. The link is on the previous page.

I love chatting to readers, so pop over to Facebook or Instagram and say, 'Hello'. Or better yet, there's my lovely Facebook group for the latest book news, chats and general book-related fun. Again, you'll find details on the previous page.

Also by Emily Harvale

The Golf Widows' Club
Sailing Solo
Carole Singer's Christmas
Christmas Wishes
A Slippery Slope
The Perfect Christmas Plan
Be Mine
It Takes Two
Bells and Bows on Mistletoe Row

Lizzie Marshall series:
Highland Fling – book 1
Lizzie Marshall's Wedding – book 2

Goldebury Bay series:
Ninety Days of Summer – book 1
Ninety Steps to Summerhill – book 2
Ninety Days to Christmas – book 3

Hideaway Down series:
A Christmas Hideaway – book 1
Catch A Falling Star – book 2
Walking on Sunshine – book 3
Dancing in the Rain – book 4

Hall's Cross series
Deck the Halls – book 1
The Starlight Ball – book 2

Michaelmas Bay series
Christmas Secrets in Snowflake Cove – book 1
Blame it on the Moonlight – book 2

Friendships Blossom in Clementine Cove – book 3

Norman Landing series
Saving Christmas – book 1
A not so secret Winter Wedding – book 2
Sunsets and Surprises at Seascape Café – book 3
A Date at the end of The Pier – book 4

Locke Isle series
A Summer Escape – book 1
Christmas on Locke Isle – book 2

Betancourt Bay series
That Mistletoe Moment – book 1
That Winter Night – book 2
That Special Something – book 3
That Summer Hideaway – book 4
That Secret Wish – book 5

Fairlight Bay series
Christmas on Midwinter Lane – book 1

To see a complete list of my books, or to sign up for my newsletter, go to www.emilyharvale.com/books

There's also an exclusive Facebook group for fans of my books. www.emilyharvale.com/FacebookGroup

Or scan the QR code below to see all my books on Amazon.

Printed in Great Britain
by Amazon